The Men I've Hated

Tinatswe Mhaka

First published in Great Britain in 2021 by:

Carnelian Heart Publishing Ltd
Suite A
82 James Carter Road
Mildenhall
Suffolk
IP28 7DE
UK

www.carnelianheartpublishing.co.uk

Paperback ISBN   978-1-914287-02-2

Ebook ISBN   978-1-914287-03-9

A CIP catalogue record for this book is available from the British Library.

This novel is entirely a work of fiction. The names, characters and incidents portrayed in it are the work of the author's imagination. Any resemblance to actual persons, living or dead, is purely coincidental.

Editor:
Samantha Rumbidzai Vazhure

Cover design & Layout:
Rebeca Covers

Typeset by Carnelian Heart Publishing Ltd
Layout and formatting by DanTs Media

To every woman

1

Something about Joseph awakened the patriarchy in me. Made me want to wake up at 5am to marinate pork chops and defrost bacon. Reversed years of apprehension about serving men in any way. Granted I was not kneeling before the 'head of the house' to greet or wash hands, but waking up in the morning to prepare a feast of note was as out of character as it got for me. I am not what my elders would call domesticated. I can live on bacon, so I am not someone anyone would call domesticated. But for Joseph? Anything. He was sad. In the way you saw in the movies, with the dead mother, the unhealthy relationship with alcohol, but not so terrible, because he understood me; and was that not the only thing better than love? He was attentive, assuring, all consuming. He had me on our first exchange and I never looked back. He was slick, dedicated to proving that knowing me was what he wanted. He messaged me over weeks, patiently so unlike most of the men who tried to access me through the internet. One Friday afternoon, he finally sent a message saying he was sure he and I would get along no matter what, in whatever capacity.

Whatever capacity. I knew better than that.

A few hours after that, we had been on a Skype call for four hours and spoken about our lives in a way I had never done with anyone before. He had so much gratitude for my time, something I saw little to no value in really. I was a student, I was free all the time. And I suppose that should have been the first red flag, because he worked and yet he was free all the time too. That was almost two years ago and we lived in different cities then, a thirteen-hour trip by road. It had been at least two months of speaking on Skype and texting before seeing each other in person, and by the time we did, I had decided that Joe was the man for me. Nothing and no one at the time could have convinced me otherwise. Love skewed my view. Bent everything to look a certain way until fatalities looked like minor imperfections. It was an inescapable disposition. Once I got myself in I was the only one who could get myself out. I knew that at my most delirious and at my most desperate, to no longer be attached to him long after things started to go downhill. Joseph's message came in one of those moments of desperation. The first after a year of zero communication. After everything.

Why do men do that?

I was so angry. I had been for a year. I was angry constantly even when it had nothing to do with Joe. I was angry at myself, at people that had warned me against him. My anger was consistent. When it was not clear in my words it was ripe in my thoughts, it followed me into my safe spaces, to my bed and in the shower. It followed me to lectures and mealtimes. It followed me to dates and experiences I might have otherwise wholesomely enjoyed. I realised very early on though that if I was angry, I never had to be sad and that was an easy pick. The music in my room was too loud. The space was small and it did not take the highest volume to feel like noise. It was loud and it made me think of Prince at a time I was only capable of being hurt about Joe. I had let go of the guilt that told me if I cried over one, I did not care about the other. I was a multifaceted woman and that could not be divorced from my love life. Nothing could compare to Joseph though. Nothing. And he loved me, otherwise why was he always trying to make his undying love known?

My personal mental prison.

I had gone back and forth on whether I could do better than allowing men who "loved" me in and out of my life as they pleased. I eventually stopped the introspection and decided I would do whatever made me feel good in the moment. I had given up on knowing my worth because it was lonely, and I struggled to understand how I could put myself first by intentionally returning to heartbreak.

I had spent most of the previous year having strange interactions and even stranger sexual encounters. It made me see Joe as 'the devil I knew'. I had been wasting time. I knew the minute he reached out I was going to have a conversation with him. I had replied, and he called immediately. Joe did not do things half-heartedly, so I was not surprised he said he had missed me and wanted to 'give things another try'. Even after not entirely speaking for a year he did not just want to check in, or find out if I still had all my limbs. He was all in and ready to be back in love like nothing had happened before. He did not want to leave Rose though. That was his catch. There was always one with him.

This is the moment the universe should have struck me down and spared me humiliation.

I was on the floor at this point. Something about making terrible romantic choices was starting to eat me from the inside out since I had met Joe. Even after smiling on the phone and laughing at all his still seemingly charming jokes, I needed to cry. I needed to weep in fact, and it had to be on the floor. I needed to physically be as close to rock bottom as I felt. I had ended the conversation at the point that Joe had brought Rose up. I could not take it. It almost made me want him more, if that was possible. And that is why I had answered the phone when it rang again not long after that. An hour and fifteen minutes was all it had taken to convince me that he would leave Rose in a reasonable amount of time and we could find our way back till then. The end had already been determined though. Joe and I would be together, and Rose would be out of the picture. There were things I knew I had not thought through yet. The stars in my eyes had not let me see past that conversation. I had not thought about what it would be like to be in another relationship with Joe. I only thought about the fact that I had him again. That a few hours earlier when I woke up that morning, I had thought about him in my usual anger and now everything had changed. I hoped I had a hold on him different to anyone else, because he did on me.

It was strange to hear his voice. To notice the small changes in tone when I knew he was smiling on the other end of the phone. This man had humiliated me, publicly left me for someone else and broken my heart into a year's worth of grief. I had rarely felt like our relationship would be forever and yet I was never ready to bury things whenever I got the chance. If anything, after my long cry on the floor I had felt peaceful and almost optimistic.

Joe valued his public image. I suppose what he valued was his politics. He was patriotic, misguidedly so. Passionate and for reasons I did not understand, willing to die for his country. He had so many important things to say. We had that in common, and that is why I had got off the phone with him and did an updated search of his online pages. People could feel what they pleased about technology and social media, but it had brought evolution in feminism, sex and most importantly love. It frightened me that our mothers and theirs before had completely trusted that men were exactly who they said they were. How did they know? It made no difference. We obviously did not know either. While we were apart, I felt it was the self-respecting thing to do; never keep tabs on his life. I had felt a sudden entitlement to it now that he had made it clear it was me he wanted. Most times, I found myself wishing the country would get better for everyone but Joseph. That he would fall into depression and kill himself. I did not think I could unlove him as long as both of us were alive, and I never felt like it was me who deserved to die. I had too much to offer the world.

Am I one of those women who loves a man with nothing? The kind we gently smile at and say, 'As long as you are happy.'

The 'as long as' had always been extremely sincere on my part because if women could not have money I at least wished them peace of mind. Taking men back always seemed much less embarrassing when they were rich. There was a reason for that. I had eventually got out of my own head enough to continue my search. It had not been long before I had landed on a picture of Joe. With Rose.

2

I did not know Rose. I never met her, never had a conversation with her, but I had spent so much time thinking about her since *her and Joe*, I felt like I did know her. I involuntarily had fragmented bits of information about her. We were only a few people away from knowing each other because we had several friends that were friends. There had been times we had 'spoken' on social media, left comments under each other's pictures and had light conversation once or twice in recent years. The day after Joe had broken up with me a year ago, a friend had sent me a message asking me why her picture was his profile picture. I had never suffered such a violent dissonance about another woman before. I spent more time than I would have liked imagining what she was like, so I could resent her even more. I knew she was in the diaspora, that she was religious and what kind of music she liked. I had taken all these inconsequential facts and turned them into her entire identity. I compared myself to her and wondered why it had been her instead of me. Rose was beautiful and though my friends had spent a lot of time telling me otherwise, I knew they did it to put my heart at ease.

What was it about her?

Joseph had left me for her. He might have told the story differently, but he had left me and hours later Rose was the love of his life. He had been with her since then. Almost a year now. And he had not let us forget it. During the year that he and I were apart I had spent so little time online. I had quickly realised that being online meant having a front row seat to Joe and Rose's love life. I did not have it in me. Rose lived in a three-story mansion with a courtyard in my head. She lived there rent free. I thought about her on nights I stayed up because I could not sleep. I thought about the dynamics of their relationship every morning. At least every other thing reminded me that she was with him and I was not. I was possessed.

Within an hour of speaking to Joe, I had gone through all of his social media pages and there happened to be Rose on every single one of them. She had been everywhere. The novelty of the conversation I had with him had worn off with each picture I saw of her. I could not identify with sadness though. I had felt the familiar feeling of Joe not telling me everything. Underselling and misleading me about the truth of what was going on between him and another woman. I only felt fury and not the kind that made me confrontational. It was the kind that made me yearn for control. The kind that would not have let me sleep peacefully unless I proved to myself being with Joe was my choice and not his. I had decided at that moment it was time to test that choice. I would see Jay that night.

3

I never needed to go out of my way to see Jay. He was available on demand, only ever one phone call away from picking me up.

He was the fucking worst!

I hated him an unusual amount for someone I had been on and off with since we were sixteen. Sometimes it was just physical, other times only for a brief moment, it was more. We had never been secretive about our little connection among friends. I looked up to his intelligence and I was happy to benefit from it where I saw fit. Jay would tell people he knew me more than anyone else. That he was the only one who understood the way I reasoned and every insecurity I had. He liked to personalise me. That was just the kind of man he was.

     Jay and I had met when we were ten years old. We had been in the same class at school. I did not have many memories of who he was when we were children, other than the fact that even then he was the loudest boy in the room. He was confident, and even after he left for a better school he remained the same golden boy. During our flings in our teenage years, Jay was competitive. Always pushing me to study harder and think about the future. It was an interesting twist of fate when we both ended up at Rhodes University. We had both enrolled into Law School and between being colleagues, ex-lovers and foreign students we spent more time together than apart. I was always one or two people away from Jay. We had the same classes, we went to the same parties, were members of the same societies, knew the same people. I wondered sometimes if he knew as much as he said he did, because I felt I had come to know him extremely well too. As much as I could have under the circumstances. I had seen many different sides to him and even when he was at rock bottom, I did not think any less of him. He was good at picking himself up. I admired that about him. It was what had led to the reigniting of our somewhat romantic connection in our second year of university. Familiarity drove our dynamic. It was difficult to explain and even more to ignore or escape, but some days I would wake up and Jay just looked different.

The chemistry was ever evolving, always overwhelming and always mutual. There were many things I knew I would always love about him. The smarts. The charm. The way his presence demanded attention. Women liked him and men not so much. They hated the same thing we all hated about him. He was always certain, even when it obviously was not so, that he was the smartest person in the room. And that was why we were never going to be together. We had a complicated relationship Jay and I. The way it worked was mostly that he spoke, and I listened. He bragged, I listened. He dictated the terms of our relations and I listened. I would say it was partly because I met him before the waking of my feminism, my enlightenment. But it was mostly because I did not believe he could be saved from himself, from the patriarchy that ran through his veins in place of blood, and yet I still wanted to claim him.

By the time Jay and I had reignited our connection we were both in relationships. Him more than me. I had known his girlfriend, Tanaka, for a few years. She was a nice girl; friendly, supportive, conversational. She was so wholesome. The kind of woman I knew life destined me ages ago not to be. Tanaka was not boring though. She was intelligent and I saw every single bit what Jay saw in her. She was too good for him. We were not friends but we had mutual ones. Close mutual friends, close enough to know when she landed in Zimbabwe, where she ate lunch, if she was coming out with us and what she was planning on wearing. Her, Jay and I had been at the same events multiple times over the years. I felt nothing towards her or about her. If anything, I had come to wish more for her. Tanaka deserved better than Jay. Not just because he was a cheater, but because he did not seem like a very good partner in any way. He constantly bragged about being her first which was uncomfortable because Jay was not fantastic in bed. He was just okay and that was on a good day. Something I only learnt I did not have to put up with later in my life.

After I left Rhodes, Jay was accused of rape. His name had appeared on a university rape list that women across the campus had made in protest against the administration's attitude towards sex crimes on campus. His accuser had recanted her accusation but that did not matter. It only mattered if he had done it. I thought back to our encounters. The times he pulled my head towards his groin. The times he would persist even after I said I was not in the mood. Jay had never violated me personally. But who he was to me was not who he was to others. I was sure of that, because the me I gave him was not the me I gave others. We all knew he insisted it was untrue. I did not interrogate him about it. Because if he had, he would not have admitted it anyway. It had been a confusing time. I knew I had to decide what I believed and reconcile with it. And for whatever inexplicable reason, I did exactly that. It had been three years since then, and Jay and I lived in the same city again. We had not seen each other in a while but in that moment, distraught about Joe, I decided that there would be a break in our estrangement.

4

I felt my heartbreak constantly. It was an unwelcome distraction, incessantly sitting at the back of my head and within the tightness of my chest. It was relentless, because even as I sat with Jay and straddled his leg under the dinner table, the only thing I thought about was Joe and the pictures of Rose he kept up for the world to see. I decided I was not going to address the pictures, because it would have been too emotionally high maintenance to do so... I was committed to carrying through with the night.

Why?

My taste for alcohol had always been limited. I did not indulge unless I had other people around me, but I let several shots of tequila burn my throat that evening. I suppose I wanted to get through the night. I just felt so tired of listening. I was tired of listening to Joseph always, and now

I was tired of listening to Jay. He went on and on about being one of the few Zimbabweans that could practice law in South Africa. He bragged about the quality of life he had, the people he had access to, the things he could provide.

"I think you might like being at my side. I am peaking."

Every time Jay spoke, it was difficult to believe the words. I chuckled and sat back in my chair, intrigued by the consistency of his character. He had looked different. Transformed rather and unpleasantly so. Jay was dark, muscular and tall. He usually looked like someone who spent hours in the gym. But he looked different that night. His jawline had disappeared into his cheeks and he had put on almost twice his weight. The city life seemed to agree with him. My mind had drifted, and I wondered why I had not seen Jay for over a year when he lived twenty minutes away. I wondered if our dynamic was on and off because we only slept with each other when he did not have anyone more interesting to do it with. I had not seen him at first because I had been contemplating the accusations against him. I did not care about whether the girl he violated took back her words. I cared that she said it to begin with. I had kept him at a distance until I battled my personal politics and lost.

Later that night I stared at Jay's ceiling while he was fast asleep and thought about whether I was really the kind of woman I claimed to be. My relationship with him had evolved into my very own feminist nightmare. All the lessons I thought I had learned stared me in the eye and asked me if I was pleased with myself. But I was not. I did not feel better about either Joe or Jay.

That had to be the last time.

5

Joseph was an orphan. He had very few friends, with only one I suspected to be genuine. His mother had died two years before we met, and he had two fathers, neither of whom were present in his life. The first left his mother while she was pregnant with him and was occasionally in and out of his life. The second married his mother when Joseph was young, and made him the subject of his violence. Joe spoke about his stepfather often. He spoke about his mother too. About how she had been prayerful but still suffered the fate of dying at the hands of a man. After his mother died, Joe had dropped out of school and moved to South Africa. He was doing small jobs at a construction company. He was writing too. He had a blog that all of social media praised every time he updated. Which was fair because his talent was undeniable. He wrote short stories too. He talked about writing more than he actually wrote but it was worth it.

Later in our relationship he would make all sorts of promises to write about me or release his book on my birthday, all of which never happened because those were the few times I actually saw Joe put time into other work he claimed was so important to him. He wrote about his grief and his battle with depression. He was one of those people who had seen hell on earth. Life was always happening to him. The reason he had dropped out of school was that no one would pay for his tuition. His relatives had abandoned him and refused to honour his mother even in the smallest ways. She had no tombstone and he certainly could not afford it. His family life was tumultuous. He had hateful uncles and neglectful aunts. So, while his friends finished their degrees and became lawyers, graduate students and others relocated, Joseph was in Alberton Johannesburg, changing streetlights and fixing water pumps. He lived with relatives, but the way he described his life, the way I saw it, he was more alone than he had ever been and that was when I met him. Loitering in a rock bottom place that I just could not see. It was not so apparent to me, but I knew he was sad and I thought he had good reasons to be.

Outside of his writing, Joe was not the kind of man who wore his poverty or his grief on his face. He was more charming and handsome than anyone I had ever been with. He was taller than most men, with light and blemish free skin. His hair was wavy and extremely black. It complimented the tone of his skin. He always stood out. His eyes were deep and made him look exotic somehow. I had known I was attracted to him even before we started talking. So were many other girls I knew. We all knew that he had a reputation. He liked intelligent girls with pretty faces and in the end, he always left them broken. He had been evasive about it when I had asked. He had been evasive about many things. Joe either gave too much detail or none at all.

Four years before we met, Joe had got a girl from church pregnant and they had his son Tendai. He spoke of him often when we initially met, and his face was plastered all over Joe's social media pages. I had come to learn later in the relationship that Joe did not see Tendai as much as he said he did. I would forget that he was a father at times. I had been too consumed in the intensity of my relationship with Joe that any other identity he had did not matter to me. I had ignored his reputation; the way he would unravel when he did not get his way, the bleakness of his potential and his low effort parenting. Joe spoke about Tendai often and it took me a long time to physically see that they were never actually in each other's presence. Maybe he shared some of the shame my father often felt when he had failed to provide for me. I only guessed this because most absent fathers in Zimbabwe would have simply been of ornamental value had they stayed with their children. They had little emotion and even less money. The nation was overwhelmed by poverty and it was plagued with fathers who did not know how to parent without money in their pockets.

I liked being with Joe, but I did not like thinking about our relationship when he was not around. I never wanted to think about it too much because it made very little sense. I was never able to justify it, and although that should have pushed me further from Joe, it only made us closer. I wanted badly to protect Joe from life and from himself. I needed to save him.

Things had happened quickly after my phone call with Joe. Three weeks after we spoke on the phone, Joe left Rose and we were at it again. I will admit I played a heavy hand in quickening the pace with which things happened. I told a mutual friend that Joe and I were back together. She was a gossip. I encouraged her to tell. And in two days, she did. Word got to Rose and by the time she tried to pick the pieces up, Joe knew he was not going to leave me again. I had no remorse. The way I saw it, she had stepped on my toes by ever being with him. Throughout their relationship I told myself I felt entitled to a stranger's courtesy just because we had complimented each other on the internet. I told myself there was nothing I could have done, something I believed to be true until the moment Joe came back. Then I knew there was something I could do. I could take him back. Another way I saw it was that she was delusional for thinking he would stay. There was something unfinished between Joe and I and anyone could have told her that. She was collateral to me the way I imagined I was to her.

Even if men were prizes, Joe was NOT!

The Saturday morning that Jay dropped me off would be the last time I saw him. I did not count on ever bumping into him again. To no surprise, the night of food and liquor had not been worthwhile because my battery had died before 7pm and I only made it back home at 10am the next day, so Joe was suspicious for days. In the weeks that led to our reunion, Joe and I had planned a weekend that he would visit me. He was back in Zimbabwe fixing phones in a small shop that belonged to his friend downtown. He was also writing articles for a local magazine, which was what he had led me on with when we caught up. I would only find out about his everyday job when I moved back home. I would also find out he was a conductor for local omnibuses, hanging out of Ford Quantums, bellowing loudly at passengers for coins while he told me he was at the office. Anyway, Joe would take the bus from Harare on a Thursday night and our plans would go on until the next Tuesday. My off-campus accommodation allowed me to have visitors for two nights, so we would stay there and then move to an intimate lodge in Johannesburg North. I had been so nervous to see him. Even more to share a bed with him. The latter was almost disbelief. No one could fuck me like Joe.

I thought about our first time often. I thought about it even more fondly in the days that led to his arrival. That and every other beautiful memory we had ever made. Joe and I had initially met through having mutual friends online. We had a few exchanges over months, which one Friday led to a message from Joe that him and I would make great friends. I became inseparable with my phone because I was virtually inseparable from Joe. It was all so familiar a year later. The first time I had met Joe was the first time I had sex with him. We had planned our first meeting for weeks too. Similarly, we had booked a lodge in Pretoria for the weekend after I wrote my final undergraduate exams at Rhodes. It was just outside of the city centre, but it was like its own world on the inside. With a spacious room and a beautiful garden in the back. We had two days there before heading back to Harare for the festive season. The plan was that come January, Joe and I would be back in Johannesburg for the next two years while I finished my law degree. That first day in 2015, I arrived at the lodge first and Joe had showed up a few hours later. My friend Tekla had dropped me off there after spending a few days with her family in the Pretoria suburbs. While I waited, I had paced between sitting still on the bed and looking at myself in the mirror on the other side of the room. I eventually heard a knock a few minutes after Joe messaged me he was almost there. I had opened the door so shyly. It was unlike me. I would always be different with Joe. Our eyes had locked, and he had held me for what felt like forever. It had only taken a few moments for affection to morph into aggressive passion. I had not planned on sex that weekend. I was on my period and it had never occurred to me until later that having sex anyway was an option.

I never got a talk about anything reproductive growing up. Periods were shameful. The first day I got my period my mother gave me sanitary pads and that was it. I had expected so much and when I did not get it, I assumed it was because I was not supposed to talk about it. That maybe it was nothing to be proud of, and hence the shame. I could not walk in a store with only sanitary pads in my hand. It felt humiliating and so did having a menstrual cycle, for some reason. So that night, after we ate, laughed and held each other the way we had planned, it had shaken me the way Joe had offered himself to my body, despite that I felt my most shameful and self-conscious. It shook me when he buried his face in my behind, because although I spoke about it among friends and made raunchy jokes, I had never had that done to me before and I really believed it took an almost idiotic amount of love to perform that kind of act. He had eased me into it. Into that and the lovemaking. He had looked me dead in the eye and affirmed me with his simple presence. He was a patient lover. He did not look in a rush or overly eager for satisfaction. His gentleness was accompanied by raw passion. The way he choked me, holding my neck down with effortless strength while he eased into me made me want to forget I had ever shared my body with anyone else. I had squirmed and frozen slightly before it all, acutely aware that my insides were not in the best shape.

"I want to." Was all Joe had said. It was all he had needed to say.

It was the best sex I had ever had, and I had never been so close to tears during intercourse in my life. Looking back, that might have been the moment I should have run. It may have been the moment before that, because after it no one could have paid me to leave that love making. We only got closer after that encounter. We had set a precedent to never use condoms.

He met my family, I met the closest thing he had to it and we shared every single day, thought and feeling together. When he was in Zimbabwe, Joe lived in Crowbrough North, a high-density suburb on the outskirts of Harare. He lived in a two-bedroom cottage with three of his relatives and their two children. They cared very little about my existence or how much time I spent in their house. That did not surprise me, because Joe had told me they cared very little about him too. On the good nights, the cousin he shared a room with would find somewhere else to be. On others, he would pretend we were not there and sleep in his bed. His living situation was worlds apart from mine. He would often say "Thank you for being here. I know you could be somewhere better."

I could have been and I was a fool for being there.

One night I had slept over on a date and my phone had been stolen through the window. On another night, I woke up to find a dark figure with a long wooden stick pulling our bags and clothes towards the window. It was like Joe's unbelievable bad luck had become mine. But I was still far too in love to care. To see the obvious. To accept that we were two people leading completely different lives that would likely never seamlessly merge. I was enveloped in his charm. I no longer knew what or who I had been before he came around. He listened constantly, bent over backwards so I did the same. He gave me the new iPhone he had been given by his friend Phill, and made sure I was safe and fed even when I sat on the old, dilapidated mattress in his shared bedroom. Nothing else mattered to me. I had never been loved so delicately.

By the time Christmas came, I knew for sure I wanted to spend the rest of my life with Joe. We spent Christmas together fitting in and laughing with my sister and her in-laws. I had never brought a romantic interest home before, but those were always a matter of unnecessary transparency. I had met at least three of my sisters' boyfriends growing up. I had started bringing Joe around from the minute we arrived in Harare, so when it was time to spend my first holiday with him, the answer was clear. On the actual day, he showed up just in time with a bottle of whiskey and meat to contribute to Christmas dinner. The day was almost perfect. As long as no one was asking me or Joe what he did for a living, we had no problem being among other people. Every time someone did, I would have a reason to temporarily disappear. It made me uncomfortable to talk about things I could not yet accept. There would be more to Joseph. He had potential. He had a plan, so why did anyone need to know he had no formal employment? The day was special to Joe and I. Despite my secret shame, we bonded on a shared vision of our own future Christmas, with our own guests and traditions. The picture was clear.

He prepared the meat on the grill and I brought the snacks and eventually Christmas dinner to the gazebo where everyone sat.

A match made in patriarchy.

I thought about our first few months often because it was the only good part of the relationship. I often felt throughout my year-long heartbreak that I was only holding onto our first special moments, because they had been the only special moments.

So why was he back then?

6

A few weeks into the year, the novelty of my family Christmas adventures with Joe
had worn off. His depression had set in. I never knew how to deal with mental health because I had never considered myself a subject matter expert of anything clinically so. I was empathetic, which apparently was not very useful. Joseph spent hours crying and self-loathing, and those few hours he said he was okay, he would disappear for days with his friends. It was never me he wanted to be around in his few moments of bliss. I had lost count of how many early mornings I had spent talking him off a suicidal ledge. He started cutting himself. Slowly at first, then more confidently. It was difficult to watch him embrace that pain. It was not the full-time empathy shift I was on that led to my emotional fatigue; it was the erratic behaviour that accompanied it.

Joe had started disappearing for days, on uncontrollable party benders, telling me he needed time alone. He proceeded to surround himself with everyone but me and had become hostile at every confrontation. Every time he started an argument, I knew it was because he needed

27

an excuse to drink and later tell me that was just who he was. On one night, he asked me if I would stay with him in a one-room house with no money or luxury. It had started as a joke which had very quickly led to accusations that I never loved him and we were worlds apart because he was the kind of person who would never win. Most of our days had become that way. I waited for him to lead conversations because anything I started could have easily become something else. I hated to upset him and I hated to hear that the relationship would never work from the person I was in it with.

Joseph began planting seeds of a break-up with me. He explained he no longer had the mental and emotional capacity to sustain a relationship, and yet in every instance I distanced myself or agreed he might be correct, he would accuse me of not loving him. He had started to accuse me of a lot of things; being ashamed of him, cheating, evilness, lying. On one night before returning to South Africa, we spent the day with my university friend and her boyfriend. The four of us sat at the poolside of her house and ate snacks while pouring endless whiskey. It had been too good a day for us to fight about anything, so when Joe's face went from merry to agitated and eventually flowing with tears when we arrived home, I was confused. That confusion had turned to disbelief after he explained that my friend's boyfriend wore Balenciaga jeans, something he would never be able to give me and for the rest of my life my friends would think I deserve better.

When I was too happy, I was privileged; and when I was too sad I was selfish, so I started to say less. Every day that I stayed with him I surprised myself. And I surprised myself for a month after that. It was during this time that Joe had planned a special getaway on Valentine's Day, surprised me with flowers, a fantastically cooked steak and bottles of wine. For two nights we checked into a hotel room in a fairly nice area in Johannesburg and I was held, touched and reassured every second of it. I was a forgiving woman with stars in her eyes. I was the friend in the group who adamantly repeated that having a ring on your finger did not change the kind of man your man could be, but when Joe got down on one knee that night, I immediately changed my mind about that. He promised to always support and love me. To be better and to commit to our relationship for life. The ring was a beautiful baguette, with one big central gemstone in the middle accented by two stones either side, in silver. I knew that Joe could not afford something extravagant, so I was suspicious of the quality of the ring, but I barely cared because it represented that he wanted me for life. It would later start to jingle every time my hand would shake but even then, that was okay.

I was a lost cause.

Not more than a month after I accepted the ring, I thought Joseph should have gifted me an ankle chain if he wanted to enslave me. He had succeeded too, but I was completely consumed in his vicious cycle and it felt impossible to leave. I could not enjoy anything when he was not around because all I could do was think about whether he was upset with me for leaving. The feeling had only worsened with time. There had been one night in particular when Joe made it clear the ring I wore on my hand, his ring, meant unquestionable dedication to him and nothing else. He had not actually said it. But he had been clear.

A friend had invited me out and we were going to celebrate her birthday in all her favourite nightclubs. I had felt so excited ever since I had been back in Johannesburg; it was all Joe all the time. I spent every weekend and public holiday with him from morning until dusk when he had to rush to catch taxis home. I needed a break from being the perfect girlfriend to the world's loneliest man. Resentment started to brew in me. I had told Joe about the outing a few days before the weekend and a second time earlier when we went out for lunch. His response had not shocked me.

"How do you know I did not want to spend time with you at that time?"

"But we spend all our time together as it is. It's just one night."

I had pretended to be casual, but I knew how short his fuse was and how close we were to an argument about me preferring my rich friends over him.

"You did not even ask what time I want you back home. What if I need you? What a selfish thing to do!"

It was too late to negotiate with him, because he had already concluded what he had concluded and it was at that moment I had decided I would go to my friends regardless of how he felt. We did not discuss it any further that day and closer to the evening I decided I would start getting ready. I had spent what felt like an eternity in the shower because I desperately needed to be away from Joe. His gloom had only grown in the hours that had passed our passive aggressive exchange. I had eventually made it back to my room to find Joe calmly going through my phone.

"You lied to me. You didn't tell me there would be other men there."

I had entered the room, started moisturising my body and thought clearly before I replied. I had not lied. Of course, there would have been men there. Men that Joe had known all his life too. Mutual friends. It did not matter. It was ridiculous to imagine myself cheating on Joe. He knew that and so did I, and prior to his latest tantrums we had never had trust issues. Fury had grown in my chest with each second that passed.

"I did not lie. You know TJ. You know Michael. You know all of these other people that you also know very well I haven't seen or spoken to for a very long time. I am going."

I had said more than I cared to because I never intended to explain myself. I wished Joe knew that if I wanted to cheat on him, I never would have bothered to go out for it. I would have just found a man to come to my room and left it at that. Joe realised at some point while I got ready that I really meant it.

"Sign me out, I am leaving!" he had said harshly. We had almost reached the sign out gate when he had stopped in his tracks.

"Give me back my ring."

I turned out without so much as looking at his face, headed back to my apartment and placed the ring politely in his pocket when we got back to my room. He had started frantically yelling and crying that I never loved him, I was ashamed of him and I cared more about drinking with friends than I did spending time with him. I wondered when I became these things because I had been fine a few hours prior, when I was catering to his needs and he had whimpered on my back.

I resented feeling controlled and I loathed being threatened with a ring. Joe eventually left me and my ring behind. His departure was followed by him sending me messages. He started by insisting that I ought to explain the importance of going somewhere so that he could understand the purpose and approve the trips. I was at peace never knowing what other terrible things the love of my life had to say that night, so I deleted the messages, had the time of my life at each night club, without his chains wrapped around my ring finger. I stopped liking the ring after that. It made me feel stifled. I hated the jingle. I thought it was cheap and I wished the rock would fall off so Joe could wither in shame.

Who should have been really ashamed here?

I started to associate it with entrapment. I started to understand that wearing the ring meant things were expected of me that I might not have been able to give, simply because they were outrageous and completely nonsensical. Joe spoke about the ring like it held the blueprint to the perfect relationship. Perfect meant every exchange ended in my submission. Me. The woman who raged against patriarchy and ridiculed unequal tradition. Who preached endlessly about the feminist way to love. About how love was not about control, and abuse came in more forms and scars that were not always visible...

Me.

I held on so tightly to the possibility of this man becoming exactly who he was when we met. Our relationship had taken me to a different place. I cried most nights and worked hard at reassuring Joe about where I was and what I was doing. I lied on most days. Lied about classes and tests and conferences. I was not seeing anyone. On most days I would not have left my house at all. I just wanted an excuse to not speak to him. It was the only time I had started to feel at peace. And yet I was sure that if he could just be the other Joe again, we would find our love. He had eventually sent me a long text message about our lack of compatibility and his need to be alone, one night a few months after the incident. I had not chased him. I was relieved I had another chance to find someone who did not weigh me down, but I was shattered because I loved him despite it all.

A week later, Joseph was with Rose. He was completely taken with her, and every piece of information I stumbled upon in pursuit of the truth pointed to him having met her during our relationship. Something about losing him to someone else made it more heartbreaking. I had gone out of my way for him for months and I spent a lot of time wondering when that had stopped being enough. I did not know what to believe. I had been played and that is how my year without him began.

Losing him the second time gave me emotional whiplash. Everything happened so fast I barely had a solid grip on memories of his first visit and the weeks that followed. The visit. That was when everything had started, well for me at least. If one thing was apparent, it was that Joseph and I were very different people. I had imagined the visit would be romantic, renewing and all telling. Instead, I had started to understand more and more, why I could never end up with this man. His jokes were stale, his ambition was fleeting and he had an air of pity around him that I could not ignore anymore. There was even something different about the sex. I wanted him to fuck the doubt out of me. And maybe he had tried. But something had stopped me from feeling that. Loving Joe felt like an irreversible action I would never be able to undo... I wanted to be with him. But I wanted him to be a completely different person. I knew it had worked for a short while because Joe wanted to be a different person too.

By the time Joseph returned to Harare, it was as if our relationship had continued from the unbearable place it had been the year before. Worse now because we were in different countries. We would argue for days then not speak for even longer. The silence had played such a big part in keeping me around. The longer he stayed away from me, the more I felt like I was missing out, the more willing I was to forgive his transgressions. I could tell he had started to resent me. He would call me controlling and suggest I had nothing else going on. Which was strange to me because he did not prefer me living my own life to the same extent. All the resentment and regret I felt towards Joe did not matter because above all that was my desperation for his love. I hated myself and I had never been more ashamed of where my heart had led me.

How did you let things get this far?

It was late in October, after days of not hearing from Joseph when I received his message.
'We are better off apart. This relationship is over. I am sorry.'

What?

7

I had been falling in and out of sleep for the week and a half that followed my second separation from Joe. I was not interested in food, or friends or fresh air; only in crying myself to sleep. When I was not asleep I was interrogating what it was about me that Joe hated so much, enough to leave me twice. I decided going to class was a waste of my time too, and having been preoccupied with the scramble for Joe, I had not prepared for my final exams at all. I was not going to revision lectures and I had not studied since my last test weeks prior to that. On the day I set my fate towards events I never imagined, I was crying in the shower and had two realisations. The first was that my exams were in exactly thirteen days. The second was that in the last year, I had never in fact forgotten Joe or stopped loving him. My sanity and progress had been aided by a distraction. Prince.

I had met Prince a year ago, a month after Joe and I broke up the first time. Evan Mawarire, a political activist from Harare, was touring South African universities. He was sending a message back to the ruling party in Zimbabwe. We loved it. We hated going back home and we hated ZANU PF. They had taken everything from us. There were so many of us in South Africa because parents were trying to get their children as far away from Robert Mugabe as possible. Zimbabwean students had showed up in numbers. Internationals too. The administration building was packed, but I still spotted him instantly. Prince was tall and hard to miss. He was rugged, with messy hair and a full beard. He was dark skinned, with brown eyes and rough looking skin. I knew I would speak to him. I had decided almost immediately that something would happen between us. I knew I would see him again during that assembly and probably around campus, but I did not like procrastination. He conveniently sat in the aisle seat a few rows from where I was headed.

"You look familiar. T." I had stretched my hand out and he had shaken it slightly startled but mostly intrigued. He would get used to it.

"I am Prince." He replied. I asked him how he was and told him I would see him around before finding my seat. Fate always found me, because I believed in it and that was how Prince and I happened.

Later that night, I walked from a friend's room back to my own. I had spent most of the night after the assembly thinking about Prince. Being attracted to someone else excited me, but it also triggered a sadness in me I did not understand. It was because the minute I thought about sex I thought about Joe. Joe who no one could ever replace. I had almost reached my building when someone emerged from the exit. For a split second I had thought my heartbreak was driving me into madness, because although I had not made out his face completely, I knew it was Prince walking toward me.

"Are you following me?" I had asked, still walking toward him. It was dark and I wondered if he had made me out as quickly as I had him.

"Not at all actually." His voice was so deep. His laugh made me smile.

"That's okay. I might be following you though." He stood right in front of me a few moments after that.

"Hi." His smile was gorgeous. His teeth were perfect. He looked upset.

"Hi."

We had stood at the entrance of my building for hours. He lived there too, and so did his former girlfriend, whose room he was coming from.

Is that not fate?

I did not pry too much, because outside of not wanting to hear about his feelings for someone else, I did not want to think about relationships. I was still heartbroken about Joe. I was still crying about him in the shower. But after three hours of talking politics, movies and music with Prince, I decided that distraction was exactly what I needed. We had exchanged numbers and spent the rest of that night on the phone. By the time I eventually went to sleep, I was sure I wanted Prince. I wanted him to care deeply for me and show me immense passion, attention and possibly love. But I did not want him to expect the same from me. In the days that followed, we spoke about our emotional unavailability and agreed our sex would just be sex and our time together would be simple. Maybe it was the certainty that nothing else would ever happen between us that led us to then spend every other night together and every other night that we were not, on the phone. Getting to know Prince was an experience. He was childish, but it was so endearing. He laughed at my jokes constantly and asked if I wanted to sleep alone every night before he left my room. The feeling he gave me resembled the pleasant burn of whiskey down my throat after a long day. I would get off the campus bus after class and head straight to Prince. We never went on dates or watched movies together because we never wanted to be romantic.

Looking back, it had never been well thought out, because instead we spent all our time talking and getting to know each other. I would comfort him about repeating a year of his engineering degree and he would ask me questions about the Law. At our best, I would be excited for the day to end so I could see him. It was like I had made a new best friend, but after the first time we had sex, it was more than just sex. It was the second time I had invited him to my room, and we had listened to music and talked about arrests and violence against activists in Harare. We had held off on sex the previous night because we did not have condoms. We wasted that night, because the first time we were intimate was the only time we had been careful.

Prince was so patient with my body. I had always struggled with orgasming, and with taking the most from my sexual experiences. I over-thought every detail until my mind had complete control of my body. Prince had little interest in fucking me like the other men who behaved like they had just been released from prison. He ravished me with his mouth longer than any other man had. It went on and on, after I reached orgasm and after the sheets were soaked after I begged him to take me. He had made love to me that night. He was so passionate in his gentleness. He kept his hands locked with mine and kissed me every time his face met mine. He called me "baby" and sensually bit my arm every time I arched my back. I had bruised arms every other day for the rest of that year.

When things were at their most complicated, Prince had asked me how I felt about him getting back together with his ex from months ago.

"Are we still talking about her? Do what you want." I had said casually before hanging up the phone. Nothing had changed for me. Maybe I loved him, but not the kind of love that could have weathered a relationship. I was going to continue to sleep with him anyway.

We had five more weeks together after they got back together before our dynamic imploded. So many things changed. Prince suddenly wanted to know my every move, as if I had been the one to take my ex back. He did not have all the time he had before, and he was always trying to get me to admit I wanted him to be with me instead. The week he had rekindled his relationship, I had seen him walking past my window and listening in on what was happening. I had been standing on the balcony of a friend's room that happened to be across the courtyard from mine. I never asked Prince about that night. It did not bother me. Maybe it was because I had never had my boundaries respected, so more than anything it did not shock me.

The more time passed, the more Prince needed me. He wanted to talk about the future and what values we shared that could have us together years after graduation. He needed to know he was the only one I wanted and that there was something special about our relationship.. He was so afraid I would find someone else. That and having to see his girlfriend around the building started to drive me insane. She was basic. I never bothered to learn her name because if she had been food, she would have been plain rice. Even walking past her made me yawn. She always had her relaxed hair tied in a sickly bun and carried a primary school backpack. She was much too boring to hate and she was the reason Prince was acting out. Rekindling their relationship made him project. He was acutely aware that each time he was with her I could have been with someone else. That made me angry. I could not hate her the way I hated Rose though. I could not hate anyone like I hated Rose.

One night, at our worst, Prince had showed up at my room at 2am. It was completely out of character and against every talk we had ever had about calling before visiting each other. I knew the minute he showed up that he wanted to see if I was with anyone else. I had started suggesting he was not the only one in my life, the night I saw him outside my window.

He sat on my bed, looking distraught. I did not like that Prince. I hated that I had stayed long enough to see it.

"Don't you think we should talk? We definitely should. Don't you have anything to
say?"

I was growing tired of being asked how I felt about Prince and his relationship. I felt invested but not enough to want Prince to myself. Despite my resentment towards his decision making, I needed the space I got when Prince was busy being in love with his girlfriend. I needed that space to cry about Joe. I wanted Prince when I wanted him. I did not care for talking about our feelings when it was almost certain it was not possible to make more of what we had.

"Come over here."

Sex was better than talking.

"Why? Do not ignore me."

He had become so irritating.

"You're here, and now I want you."

I worked hard at ignoring all the confusing feelings between us through sex. It almost always worked but I had seen it was getting harder to get away with.

"T. Stop. I am not here for that."

I had heard enough.

"Well this is what we do, so if you're not here for this then you should leave."

I stood up and opened the door for him. I was tired of helping Prince with the burden of his guilt. I wanted no part in discussing what was happening with his girlfriend and what that meant for us.

"Hey P."
"Yea?"

"Do not come back here again if it's not for sex. And do not show up without calling."

Stone cold.

He could have gone to her room if he felt so lonely. I had run out of room in my head for more sadness. I resented that she only had to deal with her man's efforts and promises while I had to deal with all the dirt that came with his internal conflict. I was the concubine, I deserved bliss. She should have been front and centre to Prince's unravelling. Why had he gone through the trouble of retrying the relationship only to become emotionally available to me? By the end of that year I was exhausted and I had to let go of Prince. It seemed easy enough. I was still grieving for Joe whenever Prince was not around and Christmas holidays were coming up. I did not need Prince. I convinced myself he was never meant to be anything even though I missed him often. He had helped me through this heartbreak..

That morning in the shower, I did not cry as long as I usually did. I left the bathroom with more hope than I had in the two weeks my heart had broken over Joe again. I thought about Prince and whether or not he was the same. I wondered if he was still with his basic girl, still living in the building we all lived in last year, still struggling with his engineering. I had searched his name in my phone and messaged him that I missed him sometimes. Maybe things could be different, and if not, at least I would have a few months of bliss. Not that I needed all that time. I would leave as soon as exams were done. My moot competition was only days away and with my exams straight after, I asked myself why I had so much time for men who had nothing to do with my future. I had worked so hard towards a law degree. I always knew I did not have the same luxury of repeating that Prince did. That many people did. My mother would not have paid for that. And as for my father.

That fucking disaster!

40

8

I left my room for the first time in a while, a few days after reaching out to Prince. I had not expected his response immediately. I may have been out of my bed, but I was still as unhappy as I could be. My motivation for leaving my room was to attend my moot competition. The exercise involved picking a partner and a topic to argue against another team in the presence of our professors as if we were at trial. I never intended on being the kind of lawyer that went to court, so I did not know why I had taken a subject that was centred on that. I had performed so poorly in that class, and that Wednesday was my final chance to fix it. I had taken an extra module when the new semester had started, because I doubted myself and I wanted to increase my chances of graduating. That meant if the moot did not go well, I had to pass everything else with flying colours. I had had an awful academic year. I spent the first half of it hating my father and procrastinating, then the second being preoccupied with Joe's return.

Thinking back, if someone had told me what my future looked like, I would have spent less time hating my father and more time trying to forget him completely. I never trusted men, based on many of my own experiences and on other women's too. I found dealing with them tedious and emotionally traumatic. Dealing with my father astoundingly so. He was the kind of man who wanted to be feared but feared the simplest of things; not being needed and being needed too much. Abraham had fought in the war. The second Chimurenga, the war that had led to the independence of Zimbabwe and displacement of the British. He had studied overseas long before we questioned prejudice and racism and eventually settled back in Zimbabwe where over the years, he had become the head of several different households and father to nine children. My father's weapon of choice was disappearing every time he could not afford to take care of us. He would completely fall off the face of the earth. Months at a time sometimes, and most recently just before my tuition fee was due.

My mother had figured it out ten years into their marriage, while she was pregnant with her third child, my youngest sister Timukudze. A few months later when the Red Cross was recruiting nurses from high density clinics across Zimbabwe, she put in an application and fled from my father and all his secrets.. She had left us to live with her sisters while she made ends meet and sent money home from abroad. Three years into her move, she started to come home frequently and on those occasions always took me to meet up with my father. But that had not stopped my blood from boiling at the very thought of him. The way he behaved at times, I wondered if he self-loathed from insisting to be the head and consistently failing to be so. His misfortune was his own. He was not a stupid man. Neither was he too poor to have no shoes on his feet. He had been wealthy once. He had many houses and plenty of land from years of ZANU PF corruption. But over the years, his infidelities, concubines and marriages had collectively given him many children. Too many for a man like Abraham. It was too much money and it was too much work.

I believed the only reason he spoke to my mother and I at all was because Timukudze was still too young to disappoint. He would wait for her to be older. Timu thought my father was a superhero, and I had always been stuck between allowing her to flourish in his innocence and somehow protecting her from the neglect I knew was coming. Abraham was the kind of man to make you feel like you understood nothing, and he knew everything. If you were not sure of yourself, you did not stand a chance with him. I imagined that was how he had kept so many women in his hold over the years. The most important thing to know about him was that at heart, Abraham was dishonest. If he was lying to someone, it was likely he was lying to himself. For most of my teenage years, he was drowning in debt, in and out of court and selling off whatever he could put his hands on, including the houses we lived in. We lived in five houses in four years and it had been pure misery.

At our best, we spoke from time to time. I knew his ways so well, but he was a stranger to me. Over the years I observed him, never quite getting the chance to learn to love him. The older I grew, the more I resented him. I had given him the benefit of the doubt when I was younger. I assumed I could not possibly understand what it meant to be an adult and they all did the best they could. The older I grew the more I had to make decisions of my own and understand what it was like to appreciate consequences. I could no longer understand the choices he told us he had to make. It was not that Abraham had never taken care of me. He had. Periodically. I was not overly grateful because we could have made it without him. His money was so deflating and almost hurtful. Because, without it, all we had between us was his blood in common.

He was trouble right from the beginning. He had showed up after three years of silence when I was fourteen years old. There was chatter and whisper from the family living room between him and my mother for about an hour before they had called me in, sat me down and told me I would be spending more time with my father. I said 'okay' and carried on watching television because even though I was always acutely aware of my emotions, I had never felt encouraged to freely do so growing up. My juvenile mind had raced, but I knew in that moment I did not trust a man who needed years to decide on whether parenting me was for him. It may not have been that simple, but it was to me. I would never call him dad. I would not call him anything.

Over the years I had gone through many hopeful moments, always followed by disappointment. Disappointment because Abraham was generous with lavish promises. It took years for me to realise this. I struggled many times throughout university because of it. I looked at Abe a lot and wondered what the women saw in him. I wondered what my mother saw in him. I imagined it was a 'different time' and he was perfectly charming before he reached his patriarchal peak. I had always told myself I would not be like the women that fell for men like my father. There was no room for romance where politics did not connect. Where empathy did not lie. I could never arch my back for the benefactor of my suffering. I would not sacrifice for the director, producer and audience of my oppression.

But I did.

I might not have been sweeping yards, going on my knees and calling men by their totems, but I did not feel like an example to women who wanted to make room for their freedom.

For their feminism.

I had only a few weeks ago shared a bed with a man accused of rape. I rationalised that the combination of Jay saying he did not do it and the girl saying she fabricated the story, then withdrawing the charge, made it okay. But that should not have mattered to me because withdrawal almost never meant anything and neither did most things that were said by men. I knew better than to believe anything said by a man, but it had started to feel like I did not actually know any better. Between Jay and being Joe's perpetual doormat, I may as well have burnt 'apologist' onto my forehead and joined a church. I was ready to be financially independent and far away from any unnecessary pleads, texts and so forth. Failing out of law school would have kept that dream further than it was in the weeks I grieved.

I looked for comfort in the thought of the extra subject I had taken for safety and found none. The afternoon had eventually taken the worst turn it could when my teammate and I had arrived at the Moot Court to find out our slot had been six hours prior. My teammate had misread the list, and I had been too preoccupied with crying in showers to check for myself or question the time he had sent me via text message. I should have. He had been so nonchalant all semester. His thirty three percent term essay mark had taken my mediocre fifty-five and plunged it into a failing grade. The entire moot class had been told at the beginning of the semester that there would be no rescheduling of moots and any student that missed it would fail the entire credit. The knot I felt in my stomach had almost landed me on the floor. The failure was not so bad. It was the disappointment that crippled me. I could not believe I had been so disassociated. That I had jeopardised my law degree for Joseph. Something had clicked in that moment that later turned into sleepless nights, impenetrable focus and long library hours leading to exams. I had sat outside the university law school for hours, thinking about how much time I had wasted being unprepared. It was when I had finally felt ready to go back to my room that I checked my phone to find a message from Prince.

I miss you always. I am on campus today. Are you here?

Right on time, as usual. Can't fight fate.

9

He looked even better than I remembered. He had put on weight, his skin was glowing. I had replied to him immediately, telling him where I was and what time we could meet. As I started to leave campus, he was the first person I saw. He stood at the stairs that led to Oliver Schreiner School of Law.

"Hi."

He saw the tortured look on my face. It was clear to anyone who would have looked at me that I was not myself. Prince was such a generous and empathetic lover. One of those very few people whose intimacy and intensity was not determined by the nature of the relationship. He had touched me like he loved me from the very first day and I found that special. I admired that about him.

"You and me. Saturday."

"Really?"

"Really. And let's not talk about anything that has nothing to do with us."

I was forward. That was who I had always been. I did not see the sense in small talk only to later tell him I had reached out so we would spend some time together. He deserved to know from the start. He wanted to. I knew he loved me or in the very least used to, and he would have done whatever I had suggested. It was hardly about love though. It was about sex.

"I can be there Saturday."

I spent the rest of the afternoon talking to Prince about the ten months I had not seen him. He had left his relationship and was 'learning to be more honest with himself.' He was still playing for the university basketball team, and he had failed another year of engineering. He was great at basketball though. He expressed that he always hoped I would reach out and he was committed to taking me on a proper date. He wanted to spend more time together embracing our feelings instead of trying to put them on the side.

Ha!

I had lied. Not completely, but I had been dishonest about where my heart was.

"You know that I care for you. Let's see how Saturday goes."

The feelings I had for him had diminished in the months we had not spoken but I had not stopped caring for him. I was fond of him somehow. That was a quality I had failed to shake about myself. When I eventually got to caring, it was almost impossible to stop. I knew I could not be with him though. He was not enough for me. He was juvenile in nature and his mind was filled with nonsense. Outside of gaming and sport, he did not know anything else. I would have had to teach him for the rest of my life and I did not have that kind of patience. I suppose it would not be a lie to say I misled Prince. I felt a helplessness in myself that needed to be distracted long enough to finish exams. I had spent too much time thinking about Joe, trotting on the brink of madness. I would later realise I wasted too much time, the little time I had, contemplating remorse about leading Prince on for the few days that led to our meeting.

By the time the day ended on Saturday I was basking in the glory of the most intimate experience of my year. It had gone on for hours. Or maybe it had just been everything that I needed at the time. I had wanted to leave my body, even if only for a moment. Something about the last couple of weeks had alluded to the deep-seated abandonment issues I suspected I had. Those and many others. And though I had a breath-taking day with Prince: bantering on pop culture, bonding on the state of Zimbabwe and the anxiety that came with having to move back, the hardships of being an international student. We rarely spoke about relationships. We could not, because Prince was not the kind of person who could have that conversation without assuming it was about the two of us. That is why when the topic had eventually surfaced later that night after he left, it had been the beginning of the end for us. The real end.

I spent the rest of the week going back and forth with him about what it would mean to make a relationship work. My truth had always been that I felt deeply for him, but I could never love him enough to commit. The conversations were of ornamental value to me, but I kept them going because I did not hate having something to think about other than Joe, except probably failing my exams and returning to a failing country. Even outside my reservations, something had shifted between us. Prince had changed. Or maybe I had been mistaken to think we were starting over. Maybe we had actually just picked up exactly where we left off. He was no longer the Prince that had provided me refuge and a getaway from life's complications. He became the complications and I found myself avoiding my phone just to avoid Prince. It made no sense because I had gone searching the corners of my phone to get back in touch with him and yet here I was completely suffocated by him wanting to spend time with me. I was unintentionally obvious. Prince went from eager, confused, sad and then the anger started. I felt resentment in his messages. It bordered on disgust.

'What more am I supposed to do to show you I want a relationship with you.'

'So does your uncertainty mean you are out fucking other men?'

'We are clearly only here because you enjoy my dick and nothing else.'

'Maybe I am just not good enough for your impossible standards.'

'T, sometimes you can be a real bitch. You aren't. But you won't stop acting like one.'

'Makes no difference actually. Rutendo and I have been talking.'

I had only briefly wondered if Prince had never left his relationship at all. I did not care too much about that though I did resent him weaponising his relationship. I never responded to him when I started to feel badgered. It never stopped him from sending more messages or calling. It ignited something more in him. He was short tempered and he did not let it go unsaid. Prince was a paradox. Even in his rugged nature he looked harmless and delicate. His exterior was welcoming and friendly but his insides were dark. He could say anything no matter how horrible and his facial expressions would not break neither would he raise his voice. He was calm in his delivery and it made me believe he did not mean most of the things he said, including the good ones. I never fought with Prince the way I did with Joe. There was nothing to fight for. It was almost never worth it for me with Prince. Right from the start. So when I eventually decided that Saturday would be the only and last we would have, I did not say anything.. I just stopped replying or picking up his call. I fell off the face of his earth.

He was just never going to hear from me again.

I was being a real bitch, anyway right?

10

The little time I had to prepare for my exams on account of all my distractions was spent sitting outside offices, always a step behind one of my lecturers. I had the strong belief that I would get more out of them about what to expect in the exams, than the few classmates I knew. I may not have been working hard, but I was certainly working smart because they had all eventually given me what I was looking for and seemed slightly impressed at my resilience. I did not have time to think about Joseph and I certainly did not have any to think about Prince, although I had found myself on a few stressful occasions thinking about the way he had touched me last I saw him. I had not had sex like that all year, and if I was being honest, it was better than anything I had done with Joseph in the short time we got back together. I was also preoccupied with packing and preparing to move out because exactly seven days after exams were over, I would have to move out to temporarily live with my older sister and stall going back home. I could not leave the country before the university decided who was graduating. And a part of me was desperate for a job that would allow me to stay. But that would never happen. I was headed back to Harare soon, and I thought about it at every instance I thought about completing my degree.

The more exams were written, the emptier the building I lived in got. South African students never had to worry about accommodation. They just packed their boxes and took them home at the end of the year. I wondered what it felt like to efficiently live out every aspect of your life. Being an international student meant nothing ever came easy. Receiving money, paying tuition, vacations where the university told us to leave so they could accommodate external conferences.. Before I knew it, exams were done and it was just Gamu and I. Gamu had been the calm in my storm for almost two years now. I had met her soon after moving universities and we had not become friends immediately, but when we did we never looked back. I had met her on social media and exchanged a few messages, following which we met up on campus and shared a cigarette. It had been exactly a month after that, that Joseph had left me and I found myself on campus, broken and unravelling. I had called her and asked to meet up and we had spent that day and every other day for the two years that followed sitting under the trees, on the green grass talking about life, preparing for it. She was my heart. Like no one I had ever met. Expressive. Unapologetic. Breathtakingly beautiful. She always understood me more than most people. The decisions I made and why I made them. She never judged me for Joe, but I knew what she thought. That I could do better, and that he was bad news. She had always made that clear. It always ended with

"Well are you happy?"

"I guess."

"Then I am happy. You will leave when you are ready."

We had been making pregnancy jokes since exams had begun because my period was extremely late, disturbed no doubt by the morning after pill I had taken after my incident with Prince. I had been feeling so off, hence the jokes which we always found ourselves making because we enjoyed reckless humour. It was the first Saturday after Gamu and I had spent the afternoon at a gin festival that my universe really started to unravel. I had so much peace that afternoon. I had drunk gin from all over the world and eaten food I had never tasted before. I saw my other friends too, the ones life had kept me from in the months leading up to that festival. It had been such a strange feeling that I had seen my best friend daily and now I would not see her at all. Unfamiliar feelings of change had been lurking for a while. In the conversations we had about the year that was following, in our plans to get good jobs. The more plans we had for ourselves as individuals, the more we realised we would not live in the same country again for a while, if ever. I had been living out of my body by the time I had to accept this. There had been too much going on around me. Too many things hurt.

"I miss you. I love you. I hope you're good."

How original.

Even with the fury that burned in my stomach as I reread the message on my screen, I was not surprised by Joseph, and I blamed myself. I had hoped he thought of me and that was why I had not blocked him. Maybe it was better to feel triggered than abandoned. Again. I felt sick. And then I actually became sick. I had felt an unfamiliar feeling of impending doom as I knelt on the cold tiles, with my head in the toilet. I knew that the drinking had not led me to that point, and as much as I hated or loved Joe, it was not him either. It had been at that moment I decided I would fix my life. I did not make a habit of blocking my exes. I was not even sure that Joe deserved to be on the blocked list. The only other person on it was Neill. While they were both vile, it was in very different forms and I could not accuse Joe of that. Nonetheless, I blocked him, right there on the bathroom floor. The next step would be to visit a doctor.

11

Neill happened in June of 2014. I met him in primary school and we had dated when we were twelve for all of two weeks, which at the time just meant sending each other a few texts a day and never actually meeting up, because how could your African parent allow that? We had stayed in close proximity with each other, bumping into each other here and there throughout high school and even after. During the winter vacation of my second year in university I spent a day at an old friend's house, drinking whiskey and catching up when Neill showed up to do the same. We had done the same thing for the rest of that vacation and that was the beginning of my hell. Looking back, Neill had never been my type physically or mentally. He was ignorant. An obnoxious patriarch who lied about the lifestyle he could afford, the women he had rejected and the people he knew.

"I do not want to make her sound bad, but I left Rugare because she just started showing too much skin. What's mine is mine, not everyone needs to see it." He would say every time I mentioned his now successful high school fling.

"You cannot fail any of your courses, because my plan involves getting extremely busy once my wife can stay home and look after the kids."

The misogyny was so deep this man had imaginary children for me to take care of.

There was a way he acted. Him and everyone that had never left the country even though they so desperately wanted to. He gave vocal opinions about things he had never tried, used English words he did not know the meaning of, and thought every woman had to prove themself to him. He hated the gays and wanted a fully employed woman who would be home at the end of each day to make a pot of hot sadza and the beef mixed with vegetables, or as he called it, *highfiridzi.*

He had been out of a job when I met him and it was absolute agony to hear about, even worse to experience it, because he was the kind of man who also had no problem with me paying for everything. And I did. I had not thought about it at the time. I had not been enlightened. I had never seen an example of romantic love growing up, maybe my idea was skewed and restricted to the things I saw in movies. Maybe I was still learning. Living outside my body and doing what I had always been told came naturally to me. Submission did not feel so bad, because I had no freedom to compare it to. On one weekend during the semester, I had taken two buses and travelled for 29 hours to visit Neill in Harare. While I was there, he had suggested a date and although things were never magical, we had had a good time until the bill came and he reached for my wallet, taken out a few notes and paid. I did not say anything. Not in the restaurant and not ever.

Who was that person?

The day had replayed in my head over and over again. I was so taken aback because I had never been so disrespected. But the part I played to get to that point became louder each time I pictured his small hands taking multiple green ten-dollar notes from my black leather wallet. I was the one who had handed him that entitlement. I am the one who had agreed to give him money for fuel every time that he picked me up. I had agreed to buy his brother and sister lunch, I had downloaded songs for him and sent him phone credit.

My resentment towards Neill had manifested in a matter of days and the twenty-nine-hour bus ride back to Rhodes University had forced some perspective into me. When I arrived back at university, I was sure about sleeping with Jay. I had no doubts. The more time I spent with Jay, the less I cared about Neill and the surer I became that Neill was not a man. I had so much to compare him to. I had grown angry, thinking about everything I had allowed myself to be talked into. It showed in my voice. In my messages. In the way I avoided speaking to Neill at all. I had scrolled up our messages to read with clearer eyes the things he had said to me in the months I got to know him for the adult male he was, not the primary school boyfriend I used to have.

'What happened to losing some weight?'

'I prefer your face with less makeup, sometimes it's a bit much.'

'I have had sex with some women who really knew how to fuck.'

'You think being in university makes you smarter than me.'

I had woken up one day a few weeks into seeing Jay and messaged Neill that it was over. I had blocked him and decided his reply would not be worth reading. And while I thought he was vile, I had only grown to truly resent him years later. When I had reflected back on the many reasons I was disassociated from my body. I had only had my first orgasm two years after Neill.

Neill was not gentle. He talked a lot about how a good woman gives it to her man when he wants it and "no" meant you just were not allowing yourself to feel how good it was. That was what he thought it meant to be in a healthy sexual relationship. Sex happened when Neill wanted it to happen and it stopped when he decided he was finished. There was no moment of discomfort, pause, stop or wait that could stop him. After a while, I had consistently pretended to enjoy it because it got him there, rather than squirming which only seemed to excite him. There had been one particular Saturday when Neill and I had had a disagreement and he had parked in my street so we could chat. We had barely had a conversation when he insisted I should let him please me so we could go back to being happy. He had torn off my leggings and pushed his fingers inside me. It had all happened so fast, it was almost like nothing happened at all. Again, I had just sat there, so how could I have felt like something happened? I had told my friends though. There were many things about Neill that I never shared with them. I had played the relationship off to be something it ended up not being, and there was some inescapable humiliation that came with it.

12

The Enlightenment.

13

The Healthcare Centre was a morbid place. The air conditioner was always set to just the right temperature. Low enough to really let the depressive aura sit in your chest. They did well in making it as close to a hospital as it could get. There was one big blue and white waiting room right next to the reception. The corridor from the waiting room led to the consultation rooms on the left and a sick bay and a bathroom on the right. I always thought the women who worked there knew better and ought to be kinder. There were magazines on the table, just for decorative purposes, because no one wanted to read magazines in there. Before the nurse had called me in, I picked up the decorative magazines in an effort not to think about what was happening. I was tired, anxious and had been up for two days because my nausea was keeping me up. I did my best to see the nurse on a Monday, but everything had been fully booked. I had also gone back and forth with myself because the university healthcare centre did not actually have any doctors. They gave free medicine to students for things like flu, stomach cramps and headaches, and for anything else they did tests and made referrals to doctors who needed to be paid. That meant if I left here with bad news, I would have a few more people to see.

I had one thought in my mind as I flipped through gardens in decade old magazines. That I would be a terrible mother. I knew that I lacked a sacrificial spirit. My mother had always told me I was selfish, and I always wondered why she taunted herself because I already knew, and it hardly kept me up at night. I started thinking about Prince again and realised my last visit to the Healthcare centre had been to set an appointment for him when he had been sick the year before. He had been so needy, wanting to cuddle and talk for hours instead of having sex like we had agreed. It had been so endearing at the time and we had joked about our inability to stick to the plan. Neither of us could have foreseen having our fling ruined by the complexity of the feelings we had for each other and the unresolved ones we had for our previous lovers. I had not imagined I would be spending my last day ever on campus in a cramped bathroom, trying to urinate in a plastic cup. I had made it out of high school without a child. I had made sure of that. I had almost survived university too, but the gods of whoever were not having it. My name was called by the nurse, and I stood up immediately to follow her. She had been much nicer than the others and it was what I needed, because if I was about to be pregnant I wanted to be spared the slander.

She had told me her name as she handed me the cup and gave me instructions for the urine sample. I forgot them immediately no doubt, because of the raging anxiety building from the bottom of my stomach. It had not been long before I sat behind the nurse's desk and watched her test my sample. That moment had given me tunnel vision. I could not see anything else except the paper-like strip that the nurse had told me would have two stripes if I was pregnant. It all happened so fast. The two stripes appeared and my heart dropped into my stomach and back up my throat into an overwhelming bout of confusion.

"I want an abortion."

I knew she knew that. She had heard it enough times.

"You have to pick a hospi…" she had started to reply.

"Do it right now," I interrupted. I knew she could not. I was spiralling. Right there in the little office at this huge university my sense of reason was crumbling, and I was thinking so much, I was barely thinking. I was not interested in being barefoot and pregnant in some poor man's parents' house. I was sure I would never live it down if I had a child. My body would go to shit and I would lose the freedom to do whatever I pleased. It was a non-starter. The nurse remained calm. She seemed to have seen her fair share of nervous breakdowns. She explained that the local hospital would perform the procedure free of charge for university students and wrote me the letter. I was no longer present in that moment. That was the moment my out of body experience had happened. I did not know any other way to process pain and that was why so many tragedies in my life were fragmented bits of information mostly made up of memory gaps. This was not just bad news though. A child at twenty-three was the equivalent of being bewitched to me. I knew plenty of people with children and I did not want their lives. I wanted mine, and I would take it back.

14

Biology is a bitch and god is a misogynist.

There were only two days left before I had to move out of my room, and nothing seemed right. I had no law degree, no place of my own, very little money, yet I had a child growing inside me, a broken heart and a disassociated mind. I was set to go to my sister's house after moving out and nothing had made me happier than knowing I would no longer be pregnant when I did so. I would be going to the hospital the day before moving out and if there was a way to go before that, I would have taken it. The truth was, even if I needed more time to gain some courage or explore my options, I did not have that luxury.

My country hates women.

I was due back home in the few weeks that followed and the abortion laws in Zimbabwe barely left women with room to breathe. Abortion was allowed, but only when the baby or mother was endangered, and when the pregnancy had been a result of rape or incest. The laws did not work though. Over the years, many women had come out to share how they had been raped and not been allowed to terminate their pregnancies anyway. Outside of that, hundreds of women had been sent to jail for illegally aborting their pregnancies. The crisis spoke for itself because the streets of Harare were full of displaced, unemployed and starving children whose parents had never intended on parenting. I had wondered why our Ministers thought legalising abortion meant everyone would get abortions. Did they know the queues for abortions would not be nearly as long as the ones for bread, petrol and cooking oil? That was the beauty of choice. It did not place you in a corner and expect you to flourish. It had become possible in the last decade to find a doctor or two who would perform abortions for the price of multiple arms and legs, but most women did not have that kind of money, and neither did I. By the time I decided when I would go to the hospital, I knew I would only leave South Africa once I had healed and my side effects were gone. The healthcare system back home was broken like everything else. I knew I was safer in Johannesburg where I could always get medical attention if I needed it.

I could not leave the country without my results anyway. I found myself slowly slipping in and out of sanity. I felt sick every morning and the small whiff of hot cooking oil made me kneel over the toilet at least twice a day. It was as if knowing you were pregnant was enough to awaken every horrible side effect associated with it. For days on end I woke up without the stamina to finish the day. I lived in my mind. I replayed my time with Prince, how I had initially met him, how I had looked for him to distract me from the fact that my heart was still breaking about Joe. I had gone completely out of my way to dig up the past and I had not foreseen it would be at my peril. My building on campus had become quiet, the parties were gone and so was the distant music and the smell of marijuana. I had no friends in the building, and the silence drove me deeper into my head. Every day I counted down to the day I would leave the hospital knowing I had no child in me. I only found comfort in my friendships. My friend Don would come the following day to take me to the hospital. It made sense to go with him. I would not have asked anyone else if he had not offered.

***

Don was truly the light of my life. Intelligent, articulate and open minded like no other man I had ever met. His levels of empathy shocked me every time. He was one of my very best friends. I had spent at least 3 days of the week with him every week for the last two years. Gamu had introduced us. Don found me sitting in our usual spot on campus one day when Gamu had not come for lectures. He had sat down, looked around, let out a deep sigh and said, "So tell me about you T." We instantly became family that day.

I could always talk to him without fear of judgement, a trait that I valued deeply in people.

The ability to connect with things beyond yourself.

He saw me through some dark academic and romantic times and I liked to think I had done the same for him. I was secretive about my situation with the exception of my immediate circle. Gamu and Don were present from the growing suspicion to the appointment with the nurse. I was not willing to go through it alone.

***

The hospital was cold and it was packed. I did not even realise a building could be both of those things at the same time. I filled out a form and sat in the line with everyone else. It did not look like it would take longer than an hour and I expected much worse. Either way, Johannesburg General Hospital was a public hospital and it was obvious. After being led to three different floors in error, we finally made it to the sixth floor which is what we were looking for. I was growing nervous as each minute passed. I had barely slept. I had Googled all the ways it could go wrong, the different procedures they would possibly do, the pain. It was as if I was watching myself doing something while being elsewhere physically. My mind was on a cross country journey in anxiety. I walked up to the reception and waited. I could see about four nurses in the room opposite the reception and they all made eye contact with me before going back to their conversation. They laughed loudly and walked around the room lackadaisically. I waited for about ten minutes before one of them came to help me. She asked for my documents and I gave them to her. She opened a book, wrote my name before returning my passport

"See you on the 2nd, be here before 7am."

The room was spinning because that was 10 days away and I did not plan on being miserable and pregnant beyond that day. Certainly miserable, but definitely not pregnant.

"I thought you could do the procedure today." I replied hesitantly. These women looked unbearable and I did not want to get into it.

"Today? You think we will drop what we are doing because of you? Why are you in this situation?" I froze. She launched into a rant in Zulu and although I could not understand the language, the energy her body let off upset me. She finished off with, "Did you come to South Africa to get pregnant?" before walking away back to the other nurses. I stood at the reception longer, frozen, eyes fixed into nowhere. The universe was something else.

I in fact could survive pregnancy and slandering.

It dawned on me as I left the hospital with Don that I would be pregnant and sick for another week and a half, outside of my personal space. As a visitor. In a place I really did not want to be. I spent the night at Don's house that night. Sick and still on the couch. I did not want to speak and I did not have anything to say. I could not be alone after being kicked so hard by life and I needed to gather as much energy as I could for the week ahead.

15

The day of the abortion was the worst one of my life. Eight days later, I found myself feeling restless and having recurring flashes of the pain I had felt on the day. My ignorant assumption had been that because I was mentally at peace with my decision, my body would have felt the same. That was far from the case. The procedure had been booked for Tuesday, and the hospital only performed a limited number of terminations daily, between 7am and 10am. Like every other government institution, I assumed the issue of time was not that serious, which I later found out was the correct assumption to make. I left the house a little after 6am and headed for the train where I would meet Don. We arrived at the hospital at 7.20am. The nurses scolded me and threatened to send me back home without performing that procedure. They dived straight into the Zulu. I did not comprehend most of it, but I cried this time. I did not understand their words but I understood the aggression. I cried because I was confused by the treatment, and I was also completely overwhelmed by what I was about to do to my body. The fear of not knowing what it would feel like to be on the other end was far greater than the fear of the actual procedure. I had never quite been at peace with my body. From the moment my 'womanhood' began, my body had always betrayed me. I was consistently in and out of the gynaecologist office, taking medication to alter or fix my period, having allergic reactions to every contraceptive and losing mobility for two days every month when my period did come. Because of this, I appreciated that things could have gone well, but they also could have been catastrophic. And it was terrifying. When the scolding was done, the nurse sent me into a waiting area. Don left me at the entrance of a much larger room than I imagined.

"I will be by the bench at the ward entrance until you come out." He said before wearing his earphones and heading towards the swinging doors. There were already four other women seated in there. The desperation I had for it all to be over meant there was no shyness or shame on my part about being there or the fear that I felt. I sat as close as possible to everyone. I had never needed strangers more in my life than in that moment. Everyone was acquainted and making conversation, and perhaps that was why that awful woman had scolded me for being twenty minutes late. I forgot their names the minute they introduced themselves and I was sure they had forgotten mine. I was wrong though, because one of them did not. She was the oldest of us all. She shared with us that she was happily married with three kids already and she had no interest in having another child. Her husband called thrice, every few hours while she was with us and each time she hung up she would smile and make a romantic remark. She also shared that she had done this before. I was so jealous of her. Not her husband or her love or "terrorist children", god forbid. But she seemed to have the least fear in her eyes. She was happy, vibrant, talkative and reassuring and maybe it was the wisdom that came with age, but she kept telling us things I knew everyone else wanted to hear. I certainly did. 'It doesn't hurt girlies,' she kept saying in Zulu. 'It will be over before you know it.' While she was talking the nurse had entered the waiting area with a clipboard and started calling us one by one. Everyone, one after the other was supposed to collect a sanitary pad and prescription medications to use after the procedure. When we collected our medication, they gave us a pill to take immediately before returning to the waiting area.

The irony of being in the most misogynistic country, listening to narrations about the joys of motherhood while the foetus in my body was dissolved by an abortion pill.

I could not believe god was this much of a joker. He was not a woman. Only a man could be responsible for this kind of suffering. I imagined the personified version of him as tall, dark handsome, mediocrely employed. The kind of man who liked 'respectable women' and responded to rape testimonies with 'what was she wearing?'. One of the girls in the waiting room was a Zimbabwean from my university, and she wore the sweater too. She was here with her boyfriend and he was outside. She was as terrified as I was and this procedure was just as urgent, because her mother was a nurse back home so the local hospital there was not an option. The two of us spoke the most, naturally. It was easier to talk about our university than it was to keep discussing why we were there. The other two were quiet. One of them was a student too, at the University of Johannesburg and the other was a slightly older woman who kept to herself and only spoke when she was spoken to. She embodied everything I had planned to be that day, but I was a coward and I needed other people to get through the ordeal. Looking back, I was not sure why I had received a tongue lashing for my tardiness if the procedure did not start at 7am. It was 9am by the time they had even given us the pills. It bothered me.

I hated nasty women. After about four hours of waiting, it was time to remove bottoms, wear the gowns and wait in a ward with beds next to where the cleaning procedure would be done. I had almost for a split second held onto the hope that the experience would not be bad at all. At my most optimistic, I thought everything might be so seamless I would share a lunch and a chat with Don after everything. I wanted so bad for the day to surprise me pleasantly and for my body to surprise me even more. I did not want to give into the inkling that I would never physically experience anything more painful. I had done plenty of research and knew some women came out so unscathed they would jog the very next morning. But others fought pain for weeks and that sounded more like me. I took the towel I had been given and went to the bathroom to change. I was bleeding. A tremendous burden lifted off my shoulders and I appreciated that no matter what happened next, the "terrorist" growing inside me was dead. Worst case scenario I would get an infection, and medication was certainly much cheaper than a child. What would I have told my family? I would have simply had to stand firm in my decision, asking for money with no remorse.

I folded my jeans and proceeded to the ward. There were way too many beds and we all took a bed immediately next to the other. I did not see any reason to do otherwise. I could not speak for the two silents and Happy Married Woman, but the university girl and I certainly needed each other. She had a caramel skin tone, a soft voice and a seemingly sweet personality. I was glad she was here even though I did not know her name. I did not want to know it. I would never see her again and it was better that way because I wanted to forget all about that day. The nurses left it to us to decide who would go when and while the procedures happened, one nurse would walk around the ward talking to us about contraception and making us choose one. Contraception was the obvious and only solution to preventing pregnancy and I suppose considering our circumstances, it seemed we needed the extra push. The politics of it all was progressive, but sitting there listening to fun facts about contraceptive pills not working while you're on diet pills, felt like the nurses were not reading the room.

Who cared?

I was also quite ashamed that at the age of twenty-three I had behaved in a way that warranted such tedious hand holding. I was not going to go first. I wanted to see the reaction of at least one of the women. Enough to mentally prepare but not too many to grow increasingly anxious. I would be third. It came as no surprise when the happy mother went first. It was not long at all, and about seven minutes   later   she   was   back.

"That was not bad at all. I told you, you will be fine."

I did not believe her and my suspicions were proven once the quiet university girl went. Her scream stopped my heart. I could feel her agony in my uterus. Upon her return she spoke to no one.

"How was it?" I had asked.

She only shook her head and started packing up to leave. I was next. I shivered because it seemed like all the heat had been removed from the air that surrounded me. I entered the room I was directed into by the nurse who was collecting us and I hated it immediately. It was small, not a very spacious place to experience trauma. There was a very narrow bed, with the back lifted to make what almost looked like a dentist chair, two metal foot bars to hold your legs up in the air, and a tray of tools. I sat on the bed and the nurse immediately said, "The less you move, the sooner this will be over. This is not easy." I lay on the bed and awaited my fate. She used what felt like a metal tyre wrench to spread apart the opening of my vagina and it was in that moment I realized I was the most vulnerable I had ever been physically. My mind was crippled with so much desperation, when I later told Don what had happened, I was unsure of the accuracy of events. Desperation to distract myself from the scraping I felt in my uterus. Desperate to leave Johannesburg

General Hospital and never come back. Desperate for the end. It was like a vacuum had been placed inside me and was swallowing me in through my private parts. I was in agony. I was crying before the first interval out of four had barely started. By the time the nurse reached into my vagina to wipe my cervix, I had made peace with unconsciousness. I had never felt so out of control of my life and my circumstances than in that moment. Completely at the mercy of these government workers who reduced this routine to tedious work. I had fallen to the floor the second I stood from the narrow chair. I felt pain from my stomach, and it went all the way to my chest. My worst nightmare unfolded.

I fucking knew it.

The nurses helped me back to the ward, composed, unimpressed and seemingly accustomed to episodes like the one I was experiencing. I was not special to them. I lay on my bed and gave myself only thirty minutes to embrace the pain. To pity myself for a short while, before walking out of Ward 156 and leaving the last four weeks behind me. Forever. I thought a lot about Prince in those moments I gave myself and it had never been clearer, the fact that I did not need him. Don stood outside the double doors of the ward ready to hold me before we headed to the train.

"Mate. It's done now. Everything is okay. You are going to be okay."

When I arrived back at my sister's home, I immediately headed to sleep. There was so much pain moving through my body parts, everything ached. I had been lucky to have Don. Before arriving at my stop on the train, he had given me a few sleeping tablets. There could not have been a more priceless gift. Before I fell into a twelve-hour sleep, I thought about what might have happened if today had gone differently. Or if I had not done this at all. The thought almost nauseated me. I was a child.

A child that did not want a child.

I thought back to a time I would have been shocked at the convictions I now held at that age. Younger me wanted a husband. She wanted children, an extended family of in laws and a life of patriarchy. But at age 15 I already knew that most men were not good people. I had seen it for myself.

16

There had been something looming in the air in Zimbabwe for decades and no one wanted to address it. I would hear the adults speaking about it and it made me uncomfortable because I was terrified of so many men I came across when I was in town, and on the road, the school grounds, the classroom and I recognised friendliness that made me uncomfortable. The first time I heard the word "rape" I was nine years old. A distant relative had been arrested for impregnating a fourteen-year-old girl from the neighbouring village.

"*Varume ava varikubata vana,* they are raping children." My mother's sister had said as she shook her head and wrapped her arms around her abdomen in disbelief. 'Baba Lovemore' had been collected by the police and the girl's family would only revoke the complaint if my cousin paid her *lobola* immediately.

"Do not ever be too friendly with men, my daughter. Many of them are dangerous."

That same year at nine years old, I was sexualized for the very first time.

I was walking home from school after playing netball. I had only just started walking by myself and the street we lived on was mostly bush. It was a new neighbourhood and ours was only one of five houses along the stretch. I was just a couple of houses from home when a man passed me walking in the opposite direction. He was a tall old man, with a scariness on his face that I had seen before.

"You are just right. Look at those delicious thighs". He said to me.

Besides him and I, there was no one else on the street. By the time he finished speaking, I had run as fast as I could towards the house which at this point was in my sight. It was not until years later that I traced that incident as my first encounter with desire.

What an unfortunate introduction to something beautiful.

I never told a soul. I knew I was afraid, but my fear was unprocessed and embarrassing for some reason. The worst thing I imagined and understood was I might be kidnapped. I did not know what could physically be done to me or how. I just knew the man scared me and I had been told to take heed, so I had a reason to be afraid.

***

It was another two years before I knew the meaning of rape. It happened to a girl in my class and Mr Chinhamo had been fired and arrested immediately. Her name was Mabel and people said it was because she was well developed, and her breasts attracted attention. I was not sure what breasts had to do with anything if they were saying Mabel was hurt and not coming back. I never spoke about that either. I did not understand what exactly had happened to Mabel and why this teacher had her in his classroom. It also came out that it had happened many times and he had started by touching her breasts during break time. The teachers at our school were not secretive. They spoke so freely about what had happened to Mabel for all of us to hear. I wondered if she would have wanted people to know all of that. It was only then that the school had invited young church leaders to explain sex to us all. That it was bad, and no matter what came, we were all to stay pure until marriage. That week we all signed papers that pledged our bodies to god. A classmate had eventually told her mother, who told the rest of our mothers, as the school should have but neglected to. My mother had come home fuming, demanding to know why I had not told her. I had not told her because I did not like how I felt when I heard about it; and most of all, I just did not know I had to.

How could I speak when I did not understand?

I thought about how if I were Mabel, I would not have wanted to tell either, because people would have said it was because of my breasts too. Or whatever else I could have had that would make a man hurt me. As the years went by, I grew to understand what a predator was. I would later realise they came in different forms, but by the time I attended high school I knew there were many ways I could be violated. It had become clear, through my own experiences and those of everyone around me, that we were always a few men away from danger. The innocence of youth did not escape me, nevertheless. I was more trusting than I was not, because nothing had happened to me.

***

Tawanda was 37 and had been working at the school going on to two years. He was the one students considered friendly, approachable and more fun than the other teachers. He was one of the few that walked around the hostels holding a beer during the weekends and lived in Harare, unlike the other teachers that were residents of Masvingo where our school was located. He frequently reminded us in the classroom that teaching at the high school was a temporary thing for him because he was in fact a businessman. That living at the hostels was convenient and that was why he did not live in the suburbs like the other teachers. After a while we stopped believing him. He was younger, talkative and friendly, which made him better than all the teachers we had. Tawanda was huge. He was a tall, heavily built man with a giant belly that protruded in any clothing. He always wore a serious face when he walked around, but smiled brightly when he was with certain people. His eyes were small for his face, and he had bright pink lips that fought with his dark skin. He had an English-speaking accent unlike many of our teachers, and he always did the students secret favours like buying them things in town and letting them use his phone. After a year of being in Tawanda's form two class, the O Level curriculum started and I left computers for Business Studies. The year after that, I turned 16 and started to prepare for third term O Level Exams. And that was when everything started.

There were a handful of boarding school students who lived in Harare. On many occasions, we all paid for transport provided by the school. On others, our parents took turns driving us between the provinces. On one such occasion, Tawanda had been a part of the group that travelled to Harare. I spoke to him as much as usual, which was not much, because I did not like any of the teachers at my school. There were no exceptions. That night, Tawanda added me as a friend on Facebook. While I was surprised, it was not strange at all because most of the prefects and excelling students had the teachers as friends on Facebook. If anything, I felt special somehow. It only confirmed that I was as popular as I thought I was, because I was not a prefect and I was only a junior. A few weeks after that, a younger junior boy delivered a large pizza to me and said it was from Tawanda. It was bizarre, yet I had excitedly accepted it, because I was in a remote boarding school with no access to fast food. I shared it with my friend Paida who was somewhat an expert of older men.

"He loves you. Just take the stuff and never speak to him."

And that was exactly what I did.

The deliveries went on for three more Fridays. Then, I received a teddy bear, food, prepaid cell phone credit and candy. By the second delivery, Paida and I almost looked forward to what was coming next. She made jokes about how he wanted me and he was my sugar daddy. I would have switched places with her any day. I found myself feeling complicit in what it was all leading to because the attention felt dirty and unnecessary. I avoided the block he taught on and changed my seat in the dining hall to no longer face the staff table.

"He is looking at you."

"He was staring at you during prayer."

"He does not leave the dining hall till we leave." Paida would always say.

I knew I did not want to be one of the girls who dated teachers. I was much younger than those girls and Tawanda was twice the age of the student-teachers they dated. I was terrified of having a conversation about the gifts and although I had enjoyed the free things, I felt somewhat relieved when they stopped coming. I had gone back to thinking about normal boys, love notes and getting on the travelling team for basketball.

***

Boys started liking me even before I knew what hormones were. By the time I was fourteen, my chest was fairly visible and my hips started to emerge. I had successfully engaged all my childhood crushes in innocent exchanges that we considered relationships. I was confident and fairly popular, so I was privileged enough to never have to second guess my looks regardless of secretly struggling with my weight. I did not think there was anything special about being pursued by men. I grew up understanding that it was the way things were and all my romantic relationships were a consequence of men following their natural instincts. There was always very little said about what the girls around me wanted. It was almost criminal to decide you wanted a boy. You always had to wait until one wanted you, then you had to be what he needed. I would later realise that was how the lives of some people would look forever.

One Friday afternoon Paida and I sat in the hostel and joked about if we might get a pizza. It was funny again because Tawanda had lost whatever interest he had in me and I could not have been happier. The usual messenger had then, to both our surprise, brought me an envelope. It was a letter and I had hated it even before I opened it. I wondered what was so important it would be on paper. Boys in my class did not even write me letters. There was something about it that was just so personal, I did not need to know what it said to know I never should have had it.

"Eh. I do not want to be a part of this." Paida had said without knowing the contents of the letter either. I felt her discomfort and I felt the same way. I had lost her as a safe space that day and Tawanda suddenly became very scary to me without my friend there to sanitise his actions. I wanted him to forget me again. The letter was typed out on plain white paper and smelled like it had been soaked in cheap, nauseating men's fragrance. I thought it was ridiculous when boys gave us their shirts with all their deodorant sprayed on them, so it shocked me that old men did the same.

"I cannot explain how you make me feel.

You rejuvenate me. I want to be part of you."

I had seen enough. I was not sure if it was shock or denial that rejected the idea that Tawanda was asking me for anything further in his letter. It was why I would not read it.

Rejuvenate him how?

I tore the letter into the smallest possible pieces, put them back in the envelope with the teddy bear that had come weeks ago, located the messenger around the boys' hostels and returned to the sender. The letter showed me that I had allowed things to go too far. I blocked him on Facebook and decided I would not even breathe on the side of the school his classroom was.

"It's done Paida. I really do not want to talk about this again."

In the weeks that followed I only saw him in assembly and in glimpses in the dining hall. And while I felt uncomfortable, I stopped being afraid that he would communicate because he did not have the chance. He eventually stopped looking at me strangely or sitting in his usual spot in the dining hall. Life went back to normal and this time it felt final. After a few months, there were rumours about him and another girl in my hostel. We all knew they were true because she would giggle and roll her eyes while her friends loudly teased her about it.

"I am just mature for my age guys." I had heard her say one day while we waited outside the dining hall before a meal. She enjoyed the attention more than me and I was relieved that I was no longer the subject of Tawanda's friendliness. I wondered why she wanted the whole hostel to know when she got pizza and when a cake was ordered for her at the kitchen. The same attention I was afraid of she had fully embraced, and it made my little life good again. I joined the choir that year because I liked to sing, and I wanted the privileges that came with it. Only O-Level Students and above were allowed to, and every year there were trips to Harare and opportunities to sing at national level. When I had been a junior, I noticed with envy that the choir girls had after-hours access to the library on the far end of the school, away from the hostels and behind the classroom blocks. They got to talk to boys while others had compulsory study and they took turns with the library keys, so they got to do whatever they wanted in there after school. I had always planned to join the choir as soon as I could. And I finally had. It was so exciting to be the one with that freedom and know if I got a crush, he would walk me to choir and kiss me before saying goodbye. Boarding school was organised. There was always something you were supposed to be doing or somewhere you were supposed to be, and weekdays felt like prison. Being a part of the special clubs or sports like choir and basketball gave us more freedom than those who did not participate. It became my favourite part of the day. Paida and I would have three nights a week of chatting with senior boys in the choir, avoiding compulsory study and hanging around the library after hours.

***

"So, are you ready for the Harare boys? They are not like these village ones T. *Ndirikuto shaya hope, I can't sleep a wink.*" Paida whispered to me while the bass singers were warmed up by the instructor, who was really an art teacher.

It was a couple weeks before the choir would travel to Harare to sing against over 50 schools in the country. It was exciting because the single sex private schools in the city were better than ours. They had swimming pools, were allowed cell phones and went clubbing during the school terms. I hated my school. I thought I would fit in better at the city schools, and every holiday I returned from my school, I made up for it by only talking to the city boys. I felt it redeemed me somehow. I was excited about travelling. It gave me a chance to see the boys some more and hopefully socialise with the ones I knew.

The closer the competition drew, the later we would be in the library rehearsing. We liked to be the last to leave so the arrangements were perfect. We would offer to lock up and only get back to the hostel just as compulsory study ended. Nothing could have convinced me that I was not having a better life than the other girls that only got to socialize on weekends, in public and in broad daylight. Later that night, Paida and I stayed in the library with five other choir members and shared our excitement about the Harare competition. We were startled when the library computer lab door opened, because it was usually empty and it was rare for the teachers or the senior boys who did computers to work as late as 10pm. A junior boy had emerged and stood at the door.

"T, someone is asking for you." He said as he closed the door behind him and headed out of the library. Everyone else followed behind him, because the surprise was enough to make us rush back to the hostel. We may not have been doing anything crazy, but we knew we were doing something wrong. Which added to my guilt about what happened next.

I leapt from the table I had been sitting on and headed to the computer lab. It was normal for the older boys to send the younger ones when they wanted to talk to us and it was flattering for some reason. Another thing I would later question and change my mind about.

I opened the door to the computer lap and my heart dropped to my stomach. Tawanda sat behind a desk in one of the corners of the room. I stood motionless and waited for what he would say next.

"Come in," he urged. I did not move. I found myself painfully aware of the distance between us and held onto the silver handle on the white door. I regretted not having questioned the boy about who was looking for me. For a second, I thought about all the things I wished he had called me into the lab for. To ask about the library keys, to get information about choir, to send a message to someone else in the hostel. Tawanda moved back in his chair as if about to stand up, never breaking eye contact. I inched closer to the door, still silent.

"Close the door behind you. Lock it." He stood up, and faster than I had caught on removed his belt and started to unbutton his shorts and take down his zip. Everything happened so fast and yet it felt like I had stood in the lab for hours. I could not place my movements, but it was only moments later that I was outside of the library pulling at Paida to rush back to the hostel. I had walked briskly in front of the other choir members she stood with and avoided any eye contact, because my eyes were watering. I was not sure why I wanted to cry or what had upset me exactly. It may have been running out of a room where one of the teachers had exposed himself. Or was about to. I was not sure what I had seen and how could I confirm it if I had never seen a penis before. It had been a blur that was not enough to tell anyone about. What would I be reporting? What would I say I was doing in the library after choir? Would I have to tell them about the pizza? I had taken it. Accepted it and shared it with my friend.

Who would I tell?

I knew the minute I gathered my thoughts I would never tell. I thought about the names that the boys at school called girls they disliked. I thought about Mabel and what people had said about her body. I thought about what they would tell my mother. They would talk about my breasts and say I took his gifts because I was a whore. I would never tell a soul.

***

That year, another teacher had called Paida into his office and smacked her on the buttocks. She reported him, and he was fired soon after.

Disgruntled, that teacher stole the email addresses of all the parents he could and sent a detailed email telling them that money was being wasted by the school, the teachers were unqualified and that there were several male teachers that were in sexual relationships with the students. After that, all the girls were asked to stay behind after assembly where we were told to come forward if any male teachers had approached us. No one did. It played over and over in my head that I had not been the only one. It dawned on me then, that there were others who had seen and done more. I wished I could speak to them.

17

There was a different air in Harare after the coup. I arrived in Zimbabwe a week after Robert Mugabe was removed from power. There was a lot of hope in the atmosphere and that placed a lot of hope in me. None of us knew if things would be better, but we had hope after years of having lost it. I was so pleased because it went hand in hand with the pace of my life. The country was starting afresh and so was I. A week after the abortion, I had received an email inviting me to a job interview in Harare to start in January of the new year. Although I wanted to be sure I had recovered , I knew it was an opportunity I could not afford to miss. The abrupt move came at the same time as my final results. I finally got my law degree. It felt unreal. I spent years thereafter questioning if I was cut out for it.

My first week in Harare was a nightmare, because my body was still recovering from the abortion, and I did not know what kind of pain was supposed to alarm me. The weeks that followed only got better. My body went back to normal and each day I woke up happier than the last. I looked forward to receiving feedback on my interview and spent my time with all the friends I had not seen in a long time. I lived with my mother's sister while I looked for my own place. On the days that I was not with friends I would sleep all day or chat with my aunt about her return to the rural homestead that was coming up. I was in a fragile place, physically and emotionally. The previous months still played in my head and I was only just exiting the out of body experience that my sadness brought about. Nothing that had happened seemed real.

***

"Who said that's the decision you get to make?
Have I even said what I think? It's not just about you."

I let out a laugh. It was a genuine laugh driven mostly by disbelief. It had been two days since my appointment at the university healthcare centre and I only seemed to feel worse with each day. I had put it off long enough and finally, against my better judgement came up with the courage to tell Prince I was pregnant. I sent him a message letting him know my period was late and that I would be going to the hospital in the next week. My relationship with Prince had almost always been on my terms and it was something we both knew. I anticipated a predictable conversation, but it went the complete opposite of what I had hoped. I experienced a Prince I was not familiar with.

"Do you want a baby with me?"

I did not think there was another question I could ask. I knew he did not, and he did not have the means to support it.

"It's not like you have given
me the chance to decide."

He snapped. The conversation had only begun, and I was already nearing my end.

"We have spoken about this a
hundred times."

We had. In our earlier days we joked about what would happen if I got pregnant. It was funny then in the glory of what felt like important sex, but the jokes had run out, and it made him unravel. I needed to be heard. He never heard me.

"I just do not think that we
should be together
is what I have been wanting
to communicate."

I was pleading at this point. I had never stared at our text messages for so long. I regretted telling him I was pregnant. There was nothing he could do for me. I wished it had all happened with Joe. He was solution oriented and would have asked what I wanted before anything else. But he treated me badly so I had no right to miss him. I had chased a boy with no range and this is what the universe had to say about it. I also doubted the decision to keep the child would have been difficult if it had been Joe's. I would have used it to leverage his commitment, but it would never work and then I would never be happy.

"I do not need to be
reminded that you do not
want me.
This is not the time to start
your bitchiness"

This time I almost fell to the floor.

> "The only reason we are still
> here is because
> all you like is my penis."

It felt like the foetus I carried was just as confused as me because I felt a bout of nausea rise from my stomach, up my throat and suddenly into the toilet where I was now facing, knees cold and eyes watering. I knew that what Prince and I had could not weather trauma or unexpected inconveniences. I knew we would have to end for good after this and the last time we made love would be the last. The burden of pregnancy was too heavy for what we had. I had also underestimated him. I had told myself I knew him more than I actually did. Prince who only swore during sex and listened to clean rap had called me names, not once but twice now.

> "Prince we both had other
> people when this started."

Why was I reasoning with him?

I was livid that this had become about the relationship I never wanted to have. I sat next to the toilet and stared at my phone. The longer the conversation went on, the sicker I felt. I did not know why I was crying. I was tired and I did not want to be pregnant. I resented the fact that I hoped Prince might have been a safe space when he found out. That we would have dealt with it as friends.

> "And yet you still slept with
> me so what does that say
> about you?"

> "You know what T? I am still
> with Rebecca actually."

Classy.

It did not bother me that he was still with her. She had nothing to do with us. I was suffering from shock because he had chosen now to tell me. I became disoriented.

Why was he angry?

I scrolled up the messages reading them one by one searching for where we lost each other. I thought back to a time when Prince had worshipped the ground I walked on.

> "I can't help you anyway. I am already in Zimbabwe.
> There's nothing I can do for you."

He was right. There was nothing he could do for me.

18

Mandla looked like everything I wanted in a man. When our eyes met my groin immediately ached. He was caramel, heavily bearded and perfectly groomed. He smelled like cologne my past lovers could not afford, had deep green eyes and a smile that could 'launch a thousand ships'. He had never looked like that before. Mandla was Joe's best friend. Well the one I suspected truly cared for Joe. They had been friends for years and at some point they seemed attached to the hip. He was confident, outspoken and easily the most attractive one of the group. He was the only one who seemed to have his life together too. He was single because he was apparently 'too particular'.

Boring.

Towards Christmas I had found myself sitting in a bar in the Harare city centre, opposite Mandla, wondering what both of us were thinking. It was not a date and we were in the company of friends we had accompanied, but the urge I had to have him inside me really isolated the space around us. It did not help that the pettiness in me had been unlocked by catching a glimpse of Joe at a club the previous week. I knew that being there meant that Mandla wanted me there as much I wanted him there. It was obvious and yet it was not. We exchanged numbers at the club that Joe was, and we spoke over the phone a few times about my move back to Zimbabwe, his work and how he could help me settle back in Harare. He was a lawyer who had graduated in South Africa a few years prior, so he was relatable. He was funny and although I knew I would not think that for long, I enjoyed the little chats I had with him that first week, so much, it had led us to the bar. The drinks flowed and so did the conversation. When home time arrived, Mandla offered to take me home. By the time the night ended, I had let go of any hope that anything could happen between him and I.

I was sure for a second that Joe had good friends.

Mandla turned the car off in the parking lot. He opened his door and came around to mine, which I found unnecessary given the circumstances. I got out of the car and hand pressed my outfit. I stood in front of Mandla for only a moment before his hand was on my neck and his lips on mine. He was not a good kisser. He pressed too hard and his hand choked too early. I did not care though, I wanted him. He was successful, attractive and I was ready to embrace my youth again. I was ready to party the way I had done during my first year in university. I intended on maintaining my carefreeness for the foreseeable future. We kissed a few more minutes and then said 'goodbye'. There was not much to address because we both knew what it meant. Mandla excited me. I knew I had no romantic feelings for him, and no relationship would ever come out of it, but he was a close example of the kind of man I wanted to attract in my future relationships. He was like the rest of them, but different.

His misogyny was almost intelligent and much less apparent, a quality I consider threatening if not dangerous in men. The ability to sound like he was making sense when he was not. We had conversations about things I did not know about and exchanged opinions on news and current affairs. He was so different to Prince. Complete opposites in fact, and that was why I was enabling the 'affair'. We called it that because Joseph could never find out because that was exactly what it was. There were a million men in Zimbabwe and I was fresh in the pond. I did not need to be with Mandla, but after the first time we could not stop. He came over weekend mornings at first, then evenings after work. We would have extremely platonic conversations, then extremely non-platonic sex. The shame of it all washed away as the weeks went by, and eventually Mandla would come straight to my house after a night out with Joseph and the boys. We spoke about Joe a lot. It made me wonder if that did not make Mandla feel guilty for keeping secrets. But he was completely detached. He made jokes about Joe and I not being done and how I obviously still had feelings for him.

"You are lying T, you know how you two are."

I knew there were bystanders to our relationship that thought Joe and I were an intense pair that always had something serious happening. I had mistaken that many times for being an undeniable love story. I was wrong.

"We are done Mandla." I would always say and leave it at that.

We were civil in public, never speaking for longer than a few minutes. There was something exciting about 'we shouldn't be doing this' sex. It was liberating in all the wrong ways, but it also made me feel powerful. I knew that Joseph was not out there thinking about me and I could not control that. But what I could control was whether I slept with whoever I wanted regardless of what it would look like if people knew. Something about sleeping with Mandla made me think of Joe more and more though, which I eventually decided was not worth the mediocre sex and the forced friendship. It had been fun, but we both knew it would not last, so when I stopped replying to Mandla and changing our arrangements, he simply stopped trying and it ended like that. I had been through so much in so little time. The time I spent fixing my problems and then enjoying my life meant even though I had feelings for Joe to let go, I spent little time thinking about that heartbreak. It was as if it had been paused and when I stopped seeing Mandla, I felt the pain I should have felt during all the months that had passed.

***

I received several strange calls in the weeks that followed. A private number had called me several times, and each time I answered there was no one on the other end. Wrong dials were a common thing in my life. At some point, my phone number had been given to someone else by my mobile phone service provider, and I received their calls. That is why when my phone rang one night in February, I switched off my phone without looking and went back to sleep. I assumed if it were my friends, they were calling me to come out and I was not interested. When I switched on my phone on Saturday morning, Mandla's name was the first I saw.

'Where are you?'

He had been the one calling.

It surprised me, because Mandla was not the kind of man to go out of his way when something was over. I also knew he had someone new and we had nothing left between us. The morning took an immediate turn, because a knock sounded on my door and when I opened it, Joseph stood there in front of me.

94

"I tried to call you last night."

Made sense.

***

I was sure Joe knew about Mandla and I. If not, it was because he did not want to know. If he was nearly half as smart as I thought he was, he should have been at the very least suspicions. One or two people had come to find out, and I did not trust anyone. No one ever kept anything to themselves. People sanitised their indiscretion with, "Promise you will not tell anyone," and then slept peacefully at night while strangers talked about their life. He looked different but exactly the same. He looked tired, like he was not better off without me. His hair was longer. Much longer, because he had grown dreadlocks, and they made him look like a child. I hated them. They reminded me of how our relationship had ended because his hair was one of the things we had argued about. He grew it out and it made him look like a bandit. I could not understand why he wanted to look as financially strained as he was.

Having Joe show up at my new apartment where I lived comfortably, the place I was only finally settling, opened a plethora of wounds. I stood there in the apartment we would have shared had he not left me three months before. My thoughts were inconsistent. They rarely matched my behaviour and when they did there was no endurance. Joe did not need to do anything else except show up, despite how many times I told myself he meant nothing to me. I wanted to stop loving him, but I still needed him to love me. I wanted him to need me so I could tell him I did not need him, but I never reached the point of not needing him. I often mistook his uselessness for helplessness, and it had landed me here. Joe stood at my door because he knew he could. He was not the type to shoot if he thought he would not score. I could not shake the thought of Mandla as the silence between us grew.

"How do you know where I live?"

"If you think I would not know where you live, then you do not know me at all."

"Have you been calling my phone from a blocked number?"

"You know I have."

Joe was an enigma. I was not afraid of him no matter how many strange things he did. I did not see him as a violent man, despite having seen him in bar fights and heated exchanges. Even after he had shouted in my face and stopped me from leaving my room momentarily the night he asked for his ring back years before. I knew at his worst he had been the driver in an accident that killed a mother and her child, but that was not intentional. If anything, that experience had made him a more careful person. I did not know what I believed anymore, but there was something about him that was inescapable.

"Let me in. I want to talk." He said.

Here we go.

19

When I finally got a call back to start my new job I had long given up. I had rushed from Johannesburg to Harare for an interview in an effort to seem proactive, and they had not called me for two months. When January had come and passed, I assumed they had picked someone else. The Sunday after Joe showed up at my door, I received a message directly from my new boss telling me I could start the next day, and to bring a laptop. My head spun so much between the time I read the message and the time I arrived at my new office, I felt nothing about Joe still being around.

It was a shiny place, with shiny suits, where twelve independent lawyers had their offices. Each of them an advocate, which meant they were trained to be better in court than ordinary lawyers: litigation specialists. Their offices were called chambers, and the chambers were elite. Each advocate had a pupil and I was one of them. I felt honoured, but I was anxious every day. Being there meant I had to have an answer for everything. On any day there was a good chance pupils would speak to board members, judges, other lawyers. We had to be ready to give solutions to problems quickly because wealthy people's empires and reputations depended on it. I worked hard from the very first day and there was no other choice. My confidence followed. My advocate took me everywhere and I was her right-hand woman. I felt the luckiest among all the pupils. I was the only woman, working for the only woman and every day I learnt something new. I shared an office with two other pupils and that was where my luck ran out.

I shared my space with Talent and Batsirai and working until 9pm three days a week meant they became a big part of my life in a short space of time. Talent was tall, skinny and beady eyed. He ironed his suits so much they were shiny regardless of material. His shoes were pointy and as clean as he was, and his face always looked like he had just woken up. He believed women belonged in the kitchen and that there were too many women in Zimbabwe for one to ever tell him how they wanted to be treated. Instead you had to be grateful and hope one would want to marry you. Talent spent most of the days talking about which girl currently was not worthy of the bright future he obviously had.

"You are lucky to be here, T. Advocate's pupils always go on to make money."

Why was I the lucky one?

"What exactly is it about you female lawyers that makes you think you're so special." He would say when talking about pursuing a lawyer, which made me think he was always getting rejected by them.

I was only shocked for the first two days before I realised I was back in Zimbabwe and that would be my normal life going forward. Whether I was in the office, walking in the street, being loud, minding my business, men would have something to say and it probably would not be nice. Talent and Batsirai, like most lawyers in Zimbabwe, had gone to the local law school. The standards of entry were high, so those of us who could not cut it had gone to South Africa, and they never let us forget it. But I was not lucky to be there. I deserved it. I had gone to a foreign country and come out with a law degree just like Batsirai and Talent despite the racism, xenophobia, the favour, the culture shock and probably having a much wilder life than them.

I was not lucky to be there.

Batsirai was short, with a big head and tiny body. I stared at him many times and wondered how so much hate could fit in that little chest of his. He wore baggy long sleeved formal shirts, oversized slacks and topped them off with ties that were absurdly big. He wanted homosexuals to be burnt and he was disgusted by fat women. Every time Talent spoke, Batsirai agreed. Every conversation he started was sparked by asking Talent what he thought about something. Nothing was censored in our working space. They spoke as crudely and hatefully as they wanted about anything and each time they made sure to ask what I thought about it. Within two weeks, I knew every detail about each of their lives and why they believed men were the heads of the house.

I hated them.

My sense of purpose came back quickly after I settled into my pupil role. I had never felt such wholesome happiness. It revealed parts of me I did not know I had. Plans, ambitions and thoughts I had never experienced. I started to have plans based on what I thought I could do for myself and how much potential I had. I let go of things I thought I wanted only because I had seen other people with them. The ideas I had about the life I thought I wanted to live when I moved back to Harare were not going to work for me. The thought of moving in with Joe now felt like giving up my financial freedom all over again. Not that I would need money from him, but he would from me and I would never feel emancipated. I found myself learning things that led to many realisations, when I started that job. Of all the things I learned, the most profound was that I was falling out of love with Joe. It was strange, almost uncomfortable and it happened in a series of three events.

20

It was not long before having Joe around started to take its toll on me. I knew the right thing to do was get rid of him, but I did not know how to say it to him. I did not know how to accept it for myself; and once Joseph was around, it was difficult to remember what life was like without him. Even when it was better. I never knew what could happen with Joseph, he was so unpredictable, but I still let him into my space. I gave him the same power he always had when he was in it. I let him come and go as he pleased, always picking up where we left off. It was not that I was happy to be with him. I simply could not physically bring myself to leave the person who all of a sudden felt like the first and only real relationship I had ever had.

I hated myself.

I knew that if it had not worked three years ago or a few months before, it would not work then. Being with him made me question every decision I ever made. It made me realise that I did not always do what was best for me, and who could trust someone like that? On most days it felt like a sex thing. There were so few men that had pleasured me well, it was difficult to let them go. Every time Joe was inside me I was sure that we could make it work. My mind played along well. It was three years later and none of the reasons that Joe and I had stopped being together had gone away. I was not the same person anymore and that was a big problem, because Joe was exactly the same.

We lay in bed all afternoon after he showed up and told me about how much better he was doing and finally had his future secured. He started off with how he planned to move into the city centre so he could have full custody of his son. He wanted to be better, he was happier and more secure. He had a steady job, writing for a foreign company that needed a constant flow of articles and content on their website. The alcohol benders had stopped, and he was 'never touching drugs again' because that was not the kind of life he wanted to lead or example he wanted to set for Tendai. I had nodded and been what I thought was supportive given the circumstances. The truth was that I was not listening and I had not been from the minute he had walked in, which was strange for someone who had let him in. I was thinking about Mandla. I had talked myself into believing Mandla and I were two adults who could do what we pleased, but it no longer felt so simple with Joe naked in my bed. My only plan was to wait and practice patience. I could not help but feel peace in the few moments my mind was consumed with childish fantasies that would come to pass. I knew that Joe was never sure about me. We would have a romance for the books and then he would disappear and be involved with other women.

And yet you kept choosing him.

That was why I no longer listened to him. I knew I was never kept around long enough to see anything happen. Joe was not a very honest man. He reminded me of my father. Or what I imagine my father would have been had he never been rich. I never took the time to discern the truth from the fabricated colourful stories and promises that Joe told me, because just like Abraham's they always revealed themselves. The first one did not need to because it was extremely unlikely anyone would trust Joseph with a child, and it was even more unlikely he could afford to rent a place of his own. I had become a master of sorts at nodding my head and listening to what men had to say. The truth about the job only took a week to come to light and prove me right.

Joe was writing a couple of paragraphs a day every day, spending the rest of his days asleep or watching television. I was curious and suspicious, rightly so because he had let me down in the past. I went out of my way to search the company that Joe said he wrote for. It was nothing like he described and maybe it was my inclination to be in doubt, but I realised it was a freelance website that anyone could write for. He was not nearly as employed as he had made himself sound. It did not bother me that Joe was working a part time student job, but it bothered me very much that he had lied about it, without any reason to do so. It was the fabrication of it all. That ten was always a thousand with Joe. I never knew where the lie started or ended. That he insisted on dishonesty is what made every lie of equal magnitude. I had not questioned him or started a conversation about his employment and he still went out of his way to lie. I scrutinised all the plans and conversations we ever had, and confirmed that Joe's dishonesty mostly consisted of half-truths and exaggerations. The lies were not complete fantasy. They were only just an alteration of the truth, mixed with an inflated sense of self because even when he hated himself, Joe still thought he was very important. It was pretty simple that if Joe was dishonest about jobs and his future, he was dishonest about us.

There was no future.

The morning I researched Joe's job on the Internet I went into a panic. I was constantly talking myself into why I could not be with him, and when the time to no longer be with him arrived, my body and soul failed me. I could not let him go. I felt a connection to Joe that transcended the physical. I was not a superstitious person, but I felt that my soul could not help but gravitate towards him. I thought about the kind of life I was signing up for if I stuck with Joe. The mediocrity I would watch and the goals I would give up, as I coddled him for the rest of our days.

That morning, I mentally prepared myself for the conversation that would take place between Joe and I when I got home. I wanted to understand why he was back and what his true vision for the future he promised me looked like. This epiphany was still not enough for me to walk away and I wanted him to tell me I was wrong about my observations and there was a reason for everything he did. I did not have a fighting chance because when I arrived home, Joe was gone. He had sent a message:

> "Gone out with the boys. See you tonight"

I did not.

***

I did not hear from Joe for another two days after that message. He did not come back home that night and he did not seem to be out with friends either. He went radio silent. His phone was unreachable and I had never been so triggered. It took me back to a room in Johannesburg where

104

I unravelled on the floor on several weekends, wondering where Joe was. At some point I had thought our biggest problem was the distance, but his disappearance told me another story. I experienced temporary insanity. There was pain in my chest and a lump on my throat for every hour that I did not hear from him. The resentment in me broke the ceiling with rage I did not think was possible. By the second night I was behaving completely out of character.

"Mandla."

" T " " W h e r e ' s Joseph?"

"I don't know."

At that moment, my second realisation came to me. Joseph consistently brought out the worst in me. I had morphed into the kind of woman I begged my friends to never be. I hated my feelings, my triggers, the emotional intricacies that made me who I was. I started seeing myself as a complete package of what the man I loved did not want. I was on a relentless mission to be the love of his life when it may have long left his mind. It dawned on me, in my moment of frustration, that I could not share my burden because I had not shared the last weeks of my life with anyone. There was an isolation that came with loving Joe. I could not have honest conversations with the people close to me about him because I did not want them to know how he really made me feel. I wanted them to love him because I hoped we would be together forever. The loneliness was nothing compared to the humiliation. I was ashamed of loving Joe more than myself. He eventually messaged me, on the morning of the third day of silence. He was unapologetic and nonchalant, so I did the same.

Why?

He said he was going through some things and it seemed he would not have a job for much longer. He was also unhappy with where he lived. His family was just as unhappy as he was. Mandla had told Joe that I messaged him and it disappointed him. He gave me a lecture about boundaries and keeping away from his friends because they were exactly that, his friends and not mine. My birthday was coming up, and as excited as I had been earlier in the year, having Joseph around suddenly made my life feel stagnant and morbid. Something about him made me never want to celebrate anything, and it was because he was never happy for me. Every time Joe heard anyone's good news, he would talk about how it would never be him. Being with him was hard.

I would not sit through another night of crying about Balenciagas.

The last epiphany came in the form of an orgasm. It was long, mind blowing and I gave it to myself. Joe and I had continued to spend time together. We spent several evenings watching television and reading together. On this night we had sex. I had blinked only a few times before it was over. Joe fell on top of me engulfed in pleasure before I had even thought about the peak of my pleasure.

"See what you do to me." He chuckled and fell on this back.

I was bored with my disappointment, I did not want to feel it at all. It was not endearing. My mind went back to the days when we could not keep our hands off each other. I knew Joe could do better. We were there because he was the best at it. As he turned the other way and fell asleep, I found myself thinking about Tende and my walk home earlier.

***

The advocates chambers were on the far end of the Harare city centre, and despite how beautiful my apartment was it was three kilometres from my office. On a good day, it took me thirty-five minutes to walk because I left home with so much time to spare. I still arrived earlier than Batsirai and Talent. In the third week of my time at the chambers I started to see the same man every day on my walk home. He had stared at me from the very first day. From the moment I turned onto the street that led me home from the office, until I walked past him as he sat on a stool in the street. I avoided his eyes and walked swiftly past him because what business did I have talking to a grown man who sat in the street?

Ha!

On the second day I walked passed him, an adolescent boy tapped my shoulder, scaring me out of one of my earphones, before saying:
"*Murikusheedzwa*, the boss is saying hello."
I had looked behind me to see the handsome street sitting man waving at me.
"*Kasi haana muromo?* Does he not have a mouth?" I had said as I put my displaced earphone back and headed home. The next day was different. I had been tapped on the shoulder only to turn around and be greeted by Tende who said hello and introduced himself. Up close, he was even better than how he looked from a distance.
That walk had slowly become the highlight of my workdays and meeting Tende somehow added a little something to it. I found out over the days that Tende went to the gym close by and that was why he always sat outside the building. He was 35 and a 'new businessman'. Tende had been a bodyguard to the vice president for ten years before retiring to provide security to less high-risk wealthy men. He had so much sex appeal. The way his shirt stretched out when he flexed and bent his arm, his smile, the way his beard fell

from his face perfectly. I started looking forward to seeing him every day for those five minutes of conversation. He had driven me home when it rained one evening after seeing me rush in the rain. I found myself wearing my earphones and pretending I could not see him because I enjoyed the way he chased me down the road just to say hello. I thought about his smile, placed my hand beneath the sheets and reached for the space between my legs. I could not get Tende out of my mind as I did. I imagined what it might be like to have him in my bed and for the three minutes that followed I thought about what it might be like if he touched me. I orgasmed. It was in that moment, lying in my solo glory, staring at the ceiling that I realised Joseph could not satisfy me anymore. My unquenchable thirst for him had disappeared and I no longer had the desire to feel him constantly. He could not make me feel the way I made myself feel.

If we never had anything else, we always had sex. We had no relationship problems as long as we were making love. We never struggled with passion and I had never met such a match, but that changed. I did not want Joe and it felt unfamiliar. He was an attractive man; I always knew that. Other women knew it too, and I saw it on their faces. Something about him had always made me think if I left him, I would be missing out, and I no longer felt that. If we were not going to be together, he would have to make it happen. I needed him to leave me. I was so inconsistent I no longer trusted myself to leave him and stick with the decision.

Even at my most certain I doubted myself.

I watched Joe fall asleep peacefully in my bed and asked myself if I had Stockholm syndrome. It could not have been, because that was for women who lost themselves to their abusers. Women that could not leave because they did not know anything else other than what the person they love has led them to believe. That could not have been me. Were we even in a relationship? I had a job, friends and hobbies yet I did not know who I was anymore. I spent years chasing a version of Joseph that never existed, trapped by opinions I had of him before I knew him. I had not just loved Joe, I had survived him. We lay in my bed estranged for three more nights before it was clear to me that I never wanted to see Joseph. I reached my breaking point, and it seemed he had reached his.

***

It had been two days since my final epiphany when I hurried past the elevator, down the lobby and out into the street. I looked forward to passing by Tende. He became more pleasant with each encounter.

"Why don't you let me drive you home today?"

He was breathtakingly beautiful, almost as if he was evolving before my very eyes. I wanted to be around him for longer, so I accepted the offer. I did not speak to him though. I did not want him to like me. I did not have the mental stamina to feel for another man. I figured if I did not say anything, he would not ask me out and I would not have to say 'no' then regret it, or worse I would not have to say 'yes'.

"Can I have your number?"

"Hmmmm-"

"Are you with someone?"

"Not exactly." I replied.

"Then?"

"Okay."

21

"I'll see you just now." Joe smiled.

"Okay bye." I smiled back.

"What's happening, how's everybody doing?" Mandla exclaimed as he approached the group. We all stood outside the entrance of the country club that led into a monthly music festival everyone loved. Joe had left home in the morning and insisted that he would not be at the festival. It did not surprise me when I bumped into him there. My friend and I headed towards a tent of our own and I wondered if I would see Joe at all that night.

"How are you doing, Mandla?"

He was excited. It was an exciting day and he looked like a vision of sex. Mandla was built like a god. His skin exuded a glow in the sun and his eyes shimmered when he looked toward the light. Every time I looked at him, I forgave him for his minor shortcomings. He wore all black that day. A black polo neck, well fitted black pants and suspenders. I did not know anyone who could pull off suspenders except him. Objectifying him came instinctively to me. I found myself staring at Mandla as if no one was around. Then at Joe, who was staring at me. I held his stare and wondered if he knew how little I thought of him when he stood next to Mandla. Something happened at that moment. I felt it in my chest, and then my stomach. I did not know that man. We had been at many festivals like that one. We used to be excited and obsessed with what we would make of the nights. We had not left each other's side. Joe had walked me to the bathroom, made sure I had somewhere to sit and kept my phone safe. Now we just stood there, about to go our separate ways. I did not see him that night. He never said anything, and neither did I. We did not speak for another few days and that was the end. I was the villain of his story too.

"I kept Tendai away from you because we will never be together."

That was not true.

"You think so little of me. I am nothing to you."

That had become true.

"You are hateful and conniving and I am done with you."

"You are the most vindictive person I have ever met T."

"You never loved me. You do not know what love is."

I might have become those things. I had lied, cheated and I was ashamed of him. I refused to be accountable for it because our relationship had become a chain of reactionary events. I had his demons, and I was not surprised my actions emulated his. I no longer had a place for Joe in my heart. I had let go of every version of him I had loved in different ways. I thought back to the last look we shared at the festival. I found it almost monumental.

I did not see Joe again.

22

I caught a ride with Tende a few more times in the weeks that followed my final 'goodbye' with Joe. I sat in the passenger seat of his maroon Mercedes at least three times a week for the two months that followed. I felt numb at first and then strangely less burdened by Joe's departure. I had anticipated worse. Foreseen days of isolation, uncanny hygiene and at least a few emotional breakdowns a day. Something about heartbreak always cracked my self-esteem too. I tried to make myself sad so I could live through the heartbreak and move on. It never came. I barely thought of Joe unless I came across his belongings while cleaning, all of which included a t-shirt and filthy boxers. It had been long since I felt unattached to anyone. Physically but also mentally. I was sleeping better and everything seemed more enjoyable. It was like nothing I ever felt, not knowing what was ahead, not feeling inexplicably tied to some idea about an obscure future with someone.

Tende and I were on our way to buy some food before he would take me home. I knew he liked me by now.

He made it clear. I was intensely attracted to him, but it was too soon. I wanted some time to be sure I would not wake up one day heartbroken about Joe. Tende was always so happy. It was infectious and he made me feel good. I wanted to preserve what we had and I was not ready to see his other side, which I was sure everyone had. I enjoyed watching him drive me around and tell me about how the smallest things excited him.

"Babe last night I cooked up a storm when I got home."

It was not a storm. It was always something very dry, healthy or both... rice, eggs, boiled chicken! But he lit up talking about it, so I lit up listening.

I glanced at my phone, ready to switch it off to avoid work, when I noticed missed calls from several numbers. My heart sank immediately because I thought it was Joe again. I did not call any of them back. I was not going to give him the satisfaction. I glanced at the top of my messages when my ears immediately began to ring. I could not see anything and for a moment I was not in the car with Tende.

> "Your father passed away last night."

I did not know why I needed the car to stop, but somehow I imagined it would make what was happening make sense. I never understood the concept of loss through death because I had never experienced it. A few of my relatives had died over the years, but none who I actually spoke to or was concerned about. More than anything, it was the grief of people close to me that made me sad. I had not suffered any first-hand heartbreak from death and I wondered if this was the time. But my heart was not broken at all. I felt nothing. It had only been two or so minutes. I wondered if I would suffer second-hand grief from those mourning my father, but I immediately decided I would not. I would watch them cry

114

and ignore them like the fools they were, to mourn a man who had done so much evil.

> "Are you okay?"
> "My father died. Let's go buy some food."
> "T…"
> "Let's go!"
> "Say something."
> "I am okay."

Death is a strange thing.

I knew his immediate assumption was that I had a close relationship with my father. He did not know, and I could not fault him for that. I allowed him into my house for the first time that night. We walked in silence, he followed me to the bedroom in silence, then we sat in silence and he did not let go of my hand.

I placed my hand on his beard and kissed him for the very first time. I had always looked at his lips and fantasised about what it would be like to kiss them. He kissed me back firmly, placing his hand around my neck. His grip was powerful. He was so strong I was sure he could snap my neck without even trying. I kissed him harder, more passionately, which made him separate himself from me. I got off the bed and stood between his legs. I wanted him and I was making it clear.

> "T. Not like this."
> "Okay."

I knew better. I knew if we had gone through with having sex, I might have avoided him for the rest of the month in some kind of shame. I did not want our first time to be strange and grief driven, but I found myself out of my own body again, watching myself do things I did want for the right reasons. It dawned on me that within a short period of time I had lost the two men that I craved love from the most. No wonder I stood there basically begging this man to make love to me. My sense of identity was crumbling. I had lost the only patriarchs I had allowed in my life and I had a biological urge to replace them both. The loss of my father meant he no longer had to be accountable for his transgressions and I was left to deal with our failed relationship on my own. I could no longer ponder on the chances of reconciliation, forgiveness and an honest relationship because the time for it had come and gone. I had buried him in my head and now I would bury him in real life. Would I dance on his grave or would I cry on it?

Dance.

I leaned on Tende and let out a soft cry. He held my hand with his left hand and held my head with his right. We were not ready for that. We barely knew each other and all our conversation had been light. I was surprised that he was still there, but there was also little room to leave. A few tears fell on his shirt.

"Do you want to sleep?" I asked.

"Yes, I do."

We climbed into bed and he held me until I fell asleep. I would not cry anymore. I had left tears on Tende's shirt and those were the only tears I would cry for my father.

23

Abraham had hung himself. His third wife found his body hanging from the ceiling lifeless and cold. He had been up there for hours by the time she found him. There was no note, no text message and no call from him. He simply decided his time was up and took his own life. I handed it to him, that even in death he had nothing to say to his children. Maybe we caused his death. Maybe our needs had grown too much to bear. I knew we were a great burden on him and yet I was sure from the minute I heard of his passing that debt had eventually caught up with him.

My mother in the middle of her dramatic rants would say:

"One day that man will kill himself. So many lies and ghosts after him."

I believed her. I was at the time only just learning all the intricacies of who my father really was, and I started to appreciate that my mother had experienced this man. After I became aware of the kind of man my father was, I wondered if my mother really knew he would kill himself or if she just hoped he would. I wondered if every woman that experienced him hoped that too. I did. I hoped that about most of the men I hated. My father, Tawanda, Neill. I imagined myself as the spirit that made sure the tassel did not break when they hung it on the ceiling or in a tree. I imagined myself holding onto the rope watching their necks break and bodies lifeless, far away where they could never hurt anyone ever again.I stood in the scorching sun, far enough from the crowd not to be seen by anyone I knew would only start crying in the hopes that we would wail together loudly in unison. I did not understand why funerals had to be so dramatic. I was his daughter and I did not cry half as loud. I was sure the loudness of the wail had very little to do with how affected the crier had been by the loss. It infuriated me slightly. I had seen it before at my uncle's funeral. The neighbours and community members had come to offer their condolences, but left my aunt feeling worse off than she was before their arrival.

They were fine to wail and cry like mad men and then go off to their homes intact, while the immediate family had to put up with comforting strangers about a loss that was not theirs. I had heard before that some tribes believed the louder the cries the more peaceful the soul rests. If that were true, it would take a full maternity ward to get Abraham into heaven. Abraham's funeral was surprisingly slow and boring and not that many people wanted to wail for him. It had not been worth the trouble. I did not hate the rural areas. I had enjoyed the monthly trips growing up, playing in the dust, making peanut butter, sitting next to the smoking fire playing with the wood that was yet to burn out, and eating food made in large three-legged pots.

The older I got the more it felt like an obligation. The visit, slaving over grinding peanut butter that we could buy in even the worst supermarket, the smoke that burnt your eyes while you sat on the mud floor of a hut while the men sat on the bench, the overly oiled food where the tomato and the onion floated on opposite ends of the plate. The relatives that made remarks about weight, the kneeling to say hello, a special "*makadii?*", clap of the hands and bow of the head to every single person in the room. The men sitting in the shade under a tree with a bottle of Gordons Gin and Mazoe Orange Crush while the women slaved away in the sun and drank lukewarm water. Those men still ate first. Their wives would eat the feet of the chicken or the bones drenched in soup while they ate two or three pieces of fleshy meat with extra vegetables. It happened everywhere and it was happening at Abrahams funeral.

He would have loved that part.

I felt an inexplicable sadness that I was ashamed of, because I hated him. I hated him and I would never get to say it. There was no one to hate. Being there also made me sad. That I had to be there, mourn him and celebrate his life with all the people I did not know, and all the people that did not know I was his daughter. The ones who expected me to know them but I did not. I did not know any of his relatives. I only knew Abraham for ten years. Ten years of nothing. The only good memories I had of him were from a time I had hope, and even those had been remembered for what they were. Crumbs. I had a few distinct memories of how I had grown to know him over the years. The first was at fifteen.

The first day we ever went to his house, he had a picture of his second wife Shamiso and children on the big stand where the television sat. His children's things were around the house and I wondered why we were there if he already had a family. The second time was months later, when I sat in his living room and watched that television next to the picture, and he had walked into the house. He had headed down the corridor and Shamiso had asked where he had been that day.

"Mai Tendai, you are too inquisitive." He had hissed before slamming the door in a way that startled us all. I never understood the arrangement, but when Abraham showed up in our lives I spent whatever weekends I was told to at his house, about thirty minutes away from our own. It was a better neighbourhood and much nicer than ours. The soil was clay red and got on everything.

That fucking soil.

Abraham and Shamiso had two boys, Garikai and Abraham Junior, and Tendai the eldest girl. She was eight, Garikai was four and Junior was barely a year old. I never liked Shamiso. I was terrified of her, so I spoke as little as possible and never asked for anything. She had never done anything to me, but I had seen what she did to my mother. The phone calls, the text messages, following her to the grocery store to threaten her about Abraham. She had showed up at our gate the year before and demanded to see my mother, who she then asked if Abraham was in the house. Her eyes were bloodshot that day. She looked like she had been crying and she looked ashamed that a 14-year-old saw her unravel. I could never have guessed that in a year I would spend weekends at her house, having five kinds of cheese. I never knew what to call her, so like my father, I called her nothing. My third memory was in an airport, not long into the weekend arrangements. Abraham and Shamiso were taking their children to Cape Town for Christmas and New Year, and he insisted I come along. At the lounge, we all sat while waiting for the flight, and the waitress asked us what we would like to order.

"Double Gin & Tonic for me, Malawi Shandy for my lovely wife, any juice is fine for the boys. A milkshake for the little lady. What would you like, T my daughter?"

"Strawberry milkshake."

"No milkshakes, you are too fat. Just bring her juice."

I have no other memory of that trip.

The last memory I had of Abraham was the festive season of my third year in university. A few days into the holiday, I received an email from the school that said my tuition for the ending year was not paid in full and I owed seventy thousand rands. My heart had dropped. The final year semester started a month from that date and I knew Abraham did not have the money. My balance from my previous school had not been paid. In response to the email, he sent me a text message on the 7th of December 2016 and that was the last I had ever heard of him.

> "Will deposit fees tomorrow"

I unravelled through the beautiful summer days, Christmas and new year. I sent messages and emails to Abraham every day. I called all three of his numbers with the international tariff and he never picked up. Sometimes it rang and when I kept calling it would become unavailable. At my worst, I left twenty missed calls before I cried myself to sleep then woke up and tried again.

I had never been so desperate.

It was like a bad dream. When the 2nd of January came, I woke up and called Abraham and it went straight to voicemail. I never called him again, once again leaving the burden on my mother to deal with it all alone.

24

Why do we sanitise who people are when they die?

It had been eight weeks since Abraham's funeral and the memorial service came sooner than I needed. The tombstone unveiling would happen and then there would be a ceremony. I thought he deserved to be left in the ground without the decorative rocks that lied about his integrity. For weeks I had thought about my opinions of Abraham and the different ways he made me feel. We had not spoken for almost two years now, so I did not miss him. But I felt that without him existing somewhere, there was nowhere for my anger to go. It stopped me from freely feeling all the resentment, much less speak of it. There was more shame around the children of absent fathers talking about it than there was around not taking care of your children. Older people were always right in the African home. I left my opinions at my city home whenever I had to visit the rural homestead. I found that the best way to advocate for my politics was to remove myself. And that was why I never had relationships with many extended relatives. I did not have to object to cooking by the fire and kneeling before patriarchs if I was never there. I had to ignore all requests, including those about contributing money for the tombstone. He was going to hell if it existed, a tombstone would not save him. I promised myself the day I left the funeral that that would be the longest I would dedicate to Abraham and his memory. From the minute I arrived at the memorial, I made multiple excuses to leave early, insisting that I had too much work that could not be put aside.

The memorial was not as crowded as the funeral. The shock had worn off and people realised they did not care much for Abraham. I did not know for certain that those who did not show up again had reservations about my father, but the crowd was too small to go unnoticed. None of my mother's relatives came, neither had any of his work colleagues. The heads that filled up the crowd were surrounding villagers that attended because solidarity and empathy was what made rural communities. I was sure that my maternal grandfather or mother's sisters would have been there even for a short time like me. I had never seen my family turn its back on duty and obligation. We had never been the kind of family that could be out in a box and fit in just one place. On some days we were whitewashed, doing things however my mother pleased, westernised by her extensive travel overseas. On others we were traditional, wearing our longest dresses and washing the hands of our eldest uncles with our knees buried in the ground. But on all of those days, we were the family that showed up.

For as long as I had known, my mother attended every funeral, memorial, church function and family gathering. Togetherness had been a big part of us, but I wanted no part in it. I did not fit in and I did not want to. I always felt out of touch with the woman I was told I had to be one day. The older I grew, the less I wanted to laugh with the elders in the hut and sniff their fermented *mahewu*. At the memorial, I was irritated by the absence of my distant family, mostly because I was jealous they did not have to be there. I became painfully aware of the sense of duty my mother had hammered into me. I resented Abe and I hated his funeral, yet there I was. Even with rebellion coursing through my veins, patriarchy thrived in me.

As I waited outside, I thought about the fact that I would never be so close to anything that involved Abraham again. I would never see his relatives again. I fully felt my presence at the last place I would associate with him. Our relationship had finally reached its end. The years of moving houses, lying to schools and comforting my mother were irreversibly behind me. He was gone.

Finally.

***

I had not spent a lot of time around older men. I found most of the ones I met to be condescending and entitled. Tende was not old, but I never experienced a 16-year gap before him. He was forty and unlike any older man I had met. They had all been big bellied, flaunting the sweat patch that greyed where their rings usually were. I did not understand the trouble of taking them off when it rarely mattered to anyone that they were married. They never denied it themselves, so maybe it was a moral high ground of sorts. It was of no significance whether a man was married in Harare. They liked young girls and young girls liked luxurious experiences. They had married the women who would make the best wives and left the loves of their lives, the rebellious ones, the bad bitches for the other lives they led. They chased youthful thrills then slept at their lovers' apartments that they paid for, furnished and maintained.

There was no need to pick the poor men in a country where struggle thrived. The single ones with less money were equally disappointing in their own ways, and it was much better to be with a man who could pay the pain away.

The thought of ending up with a man who had the mental stamina to commit to cheating on me for the rest of his life scared me. I had avoided Tende for so long when we first met because he was god-like. He was the centre of attention wherever he went and the most handsome man in the room at almost any given time. He was definitely the most attractive man I had ever been with. We spent every other day together since the funeral.

I looked forward to the end of my work days because it meant I got to see Tende. We planned our dinners as we drove home, then spent our nights watching movies and talking about our days. On some days we drank wine, because I had so much to learn and Tende had a lot to teach. He made me taste different kinds and tried to convince me that each one was better than the last. He would go on and on about the origin of the wine and how it was 'spicy' or 'just the right age', and I would sip, listen and nod then insist they all tasted the same. I enjoyed tasting wine with him even when it was all the same.

We had different tastes in films, music and food and deciding on any of those was always an event, a bonding time of sorts. It was only a small part of the time we spent together, but it was special to me. I was suddenly ever evolving, something I valued because I had spent so many years going back and forth with the same man. Tende and I were not exactly a couple though. I spent a lot of time avoiding having conversations that would make our relationship official. Things moved slowly over the months that followed Abraham's death. I knew that I had feelings for him, but my reservations about romance and vulnerability were loud and unforgiving. I was painfully aware of the fact that Tende had been there through the passing of my father and present during the time Joe and I ended. I wanted to be sure about what we had. That was why we had not had sex. It was as if we were the best of friends. I felt so close to him,

I was terrified about what more there was to feel. I never tried sex with him again since the night I heard about my father, and neither had he.

"I want you more than anything." He would say when things got heated between us. The sexual tension between us was all consuming in those moments and after months of waiting, I almost needed the sex. I needed to show Tende how he made me feel. Something about closing a chapter with Abraham made me feel courageous. I almost knew, as Tende picked me up from the memorial that I was ready.

Ready for him.

***

"It's time to talk about us T."
"Or it's time for alcohol."
We sat in Tende's bedroom with our legs entwined, wine glasses in hand, another bottle unopened as soul music played in the background. We were on our second bottle of the night, talking about different restaurants in Harare we wanted to try together. The day had such great meaning to it. I would later learn that the true face of death shows itself when you truly lose a loved one. I had not yet felt loss. Abraham had just gone further away. I knew it was in my head but I was sure Tende's beard was shiner than usual, and his touch was sending my head to elevated places. He touched my face and looked right at me.

"I want to be with you. Officially. I do not want the blurred lines."

He had a gentleness about him. I had wanted to be with him from the beginning of the little friendship we had worked on. He did not need to ask but I loved that he did. He knew exactly what he wanted from me and was ready to give the same.

"Okay."

I replied. His eyes lit up and we smiled at each other for what felt like eternity.

"Okay."

He said back. He leaned forward and kissed me softly. I hoped that he loved me because I was sure that was what I felt for him. We put our glasses down and only focused on each other. We kissed passionately as his hand gripped my neck and my hand firmly held his ribcage.

"I think we have waited long enough to be honest."

Too long.

I laughed hard because I agreed. I was not the waiting kind of woman. I liked what I liked and sex allowed me to share my feelings without talking about them.

"I love you T." He did not break eye contact. My heart fell into my stomach.

I was so adamant about taking things slow, but I was so far gone already it no longer mattered. I was in too deep. I adored Tende and I had not imagined I would meet a man on the side of the road immediately and that would be it.

"I love you."

***

I had no doubt in my mind that our first time would be mind-blowing even if it was not. We had waited so long, shared so many feelings my mind decided from the beginning that it would be perfect. Tende and I had discussed the nature of our connection and what we imagined our sex would be like. I learned very early in our friendship that over the years Tende had lost many friends to HIV/AIDS. He talked about his generation being the one that tested people with their eyes and decided sex with beautiful women excluded them from risk. A few weeks prior we had made a date of testing ourselves at home and choking back shots of whiskey so we could freely talk about what we liked in the bedroom. I initiated it because every time I saw him I was not sure how much longer I could go without climbing him and I wanted that moment to be perfect. I did not want it to be ruined by talking about sexual health when we could do it before. Being with Tende was different in every way. We spent a lot of time talking about doing things together and we spent more following through with those things. Longevity was new to me.

***

We were eager for each other. We had been patient and we deserved that night. He moved towards me and took me into his arms, firmly putting his lips on mine. I wore a dress shirt with nothing underneath.

"Are you okay? May I? Do you like that?" He asked every few moments before carefully removing the buttons on the shirt.

There was depth and disbelief in Tende's eyes when he looked at my body. He seemed almost in awe that he could be so lucky. It made me feel sexy. Like there was nowhere else I wanted to be. His strength was difficult to ignore and compared to him, I was tiny. He lifted me, guided my legs around his waist and placed me effortlessly onto the bed. His body covered all of mine when he lay me down. He stroked my forehead with his thumb as he kissed it and whispered how deeply he felt for me. Tende was unbelievably shy for someone who looked the way he did. There was no hesitation in the way he held me or positioned my body, but every time I told him I liked something or called him daddy he blushed tremendously before saying, "Me?" There were so many little things about him I enjoyed.

"I want to have you forever!" He exclaimed as he orgasmed that night. He hardened his grip around my waist.

25

I decided from the beginning that what I had with Tende would be different from how I knew love. I did not want it to be about my last relationships or whatever trauma I had. I wanted it far from the places and things I usually liked, so it always felt new. We had our own thing, Tende and I. He made me feel chosen. I found it dangerous to feel that kind of security in men because it deprived me of some of my identity. I felt like I was giving in to the idea that being loved by a man made me more valuable. But the way Tende loved me was so unfamiliar to me. There was intention in the way he took care of me. I had never been taken care of financially or mentally, but it was not just that. He took care of me in the ways that mattered. He got medical aid for me, paid any extra costs when I went to the doctor, medication included. He had groceries delivered to me every month and paid for all my cell phone costs. It was not just the money, there was attention to detail in the smaller things too. The way he made sure I always had a way to get home from work, even though it was walking distance, the interest he took in my interests, remembering the storylines of the co-workers I wanted to forget and watching my favourite shows that he did not understand. There was a gentleness about Tende, who was always present but never overwhelming. We could sit in silence for hours, but we also spent many nights having three-hour conversations about politics, books, movies and gossip about the people in our lives.

The conversations between my mother and I shifted. She evolved past jokes about if I had eaten in a ladylike manner during our date, to asking if I was ready to live with a man or whether Tende wanted children.

"I am not getting married."

I always reminded my mother that she would only attend one daughter's wedding. I could not lead her on and disappoint her. It would have been better to pleasantly surprise her. She also evolved past arguing with me about it and insisted that I find someone and have children of my own.

Not a chance.

She surprised me sometimes. Progressive in her own ways. But my mother and I had different bars and I could not take her romantic advice because I wanted nothing to do with the kind of men she had loved or the relationships she had been in. She frowned on my radical ideas and over the years had said things like:

"Who will marry you if you are this type of woman?"
"Men do not like women like that."

Who the fuck cared what they liked?

She always insisted I be a little less of who I really was and I never understood why. It did not bother me. She did not know me, but I had accepted that. Among the things that could not be changed about her, my mother decided that she liked Tende and he was my future. He checked on her regularly and they had regular phone conversations. He became a consistent part of my life until he became family.

The first time Tende and I had a fight, something shifted in our relationship. Something good. It was as if realising for the first time that I wanted to be with him. It was not that I had not taken him or our relationship seriously, but there was a natural guard that came in new relationships that only went away at the other side of uncomfortable conversations. The worst thing about our disagreement was that it was not even about us. Tende's youngest brother, Blessing, had called during one of our nights in to seek advice about his girlfriend who would not take the morning after pill. He called her a gold digger and said she could not be trusted for not insisting on a condom in the first place.

"She's a thot so I fucked her."

As if she did not fuck him back.

Tende did not know what a 'thot' was. He was too old by the time men started calling women That Hoe Over There. Blessing was closer to my age than Tende. He was 19 years old, a second-year university student and Tende did anything for him. It had not been long into our relationship that I had become a part of their late-night advice sessions, especially if it was about women. I had to fight the patriarchy from the inside. Tende mostly listened and gave a short word before hanging up and getting back to me.

"Well you can tell her if she wants to be a single mother in this crumbling economy that is up to her. She will not see a cent from us."

I had immediately withdrawn from the conversation and waited for Tende to get off the phone before I asked, "So if I did not want the morning after pill I would be a single mother then?"

"Why would you not take it if you can prevent something neither of us wants?"

"There are many reasons women do not want to take the pill."

"Besides money?"

"If I refused to take it, would you say I was trying to trap you."

"Well we will never have to find out will we?"

"Well leave then if I am just here for your money."

***

Maybe I was damaged and distrusting because of my past relationships. Or maybe my tendency to be suspicious would later protect me from believing things could never happen to me. Either way, I waited for months for Tende to transform into someone I could not love or in the very least show me his ugly side.

"Too good to be true!" I would tease when I shared my thoughts with him about his ugly side.

There were few things I enjoyed more than Tende's personal politics. I would not have gone as far as calling him an advocate, or even a feminist. But he minded his business and hated those who did not. Every take he had from sexuality to gender rights was premised on the simple solution that everyone should mind their own business, and lack of empathy made anyone morally corrupt.

Which did not apply to working for the party that killed citizens for decades apparently.

His take on justice was simple, but it was enough for me. While it would have been nice, I did not need a man who waved his fists with me and took to the streets in revolution or recited feminist theory. I just needed one who understood why I was everything I was. He knew from very early on I was not interested in marriage. It was not a problem with him and I imagined that was why he never fixated on it the way most Zimbabwean men did. Even in my perpetual skepticism, I started to settle well with the idea of a long-term relationship. I embraced my dependence on Tende and he never let me down.

26

"That's one hell of a glow sis."

I looked up from my phone to see Takunda standing a few meters from me, hands crossed above her stomach and suitcases by her side. I felt a deep feeling of unfamiliarity looking at my sister in the centre of the airport. I had not seen her in nearly two years, since leaving her house in Johannesburg after university. We spoke frequently over the phone and recently when she had called to say she was visiting for a few days to sort out her children's birth certificates. Her and I disagreed about most things, and at the top of that list was things to tell and not tell our mother. They were closer than my mother and me. They were also closer than she and I. They were equally unaware of who I was and comfortable in their oblivion. I always felt like a stranger growing up. In the years that led to my enlightenment I realised I loved the people around me, but I did not like them. I detested their politics and I resented the ways they did not see me. Whenever I fought with relatives, I was happy to continue my life and act like they did not exist. We did not have anything to speak about.

When Takunda reached out I was excited. She would finally get the chance to spend my money and sleep under my roof, the way I had done with her for most of my university years. I worked most days and slept early at night, so I had taken one day off to pick her up and make her a nice dinner.

"Hey there!" I replied and fought back a smile. I had been hearing that word a lot. And I indeed had been glowing. It was the glow of a woman who had started exceeding her own expectations.

Bliss.

There was confidence that came with growing at work. I made more acquaintances and learned new hobbies. Tende and I made plans for our future every day that were about to come into being. I looked at houses and furniture with him knowing I did not have a penny to my name.

"As long as I am breathing you are sorted T," he would say when I reminded him of that as we scrolled Property24 and PropertyZW. I had decided everything would be okay.

I hugged my sister.

"Whatever is on your skin, I want it." She said as we pulled apart. She was glowing too.

I helped her with her bags and we headed to my apartment. We sat in the kitchen as I peeled carrots while she watched me.

"So where is Tendekai?" She eventually broke the silence. I had to let out a laugh.

"Who?"

"You know your Mother cannot keep a secret."

Not endearing.

"Uganda, Ghana then Joburg. He will be back in a week and a half."

Tende's travelling had become the uncomfortable conversation of our relationship. A year into our relationship he had gone back to doing security detail because entrepreneurship was getting 'boring' for him. That, and the economy got worse with each day. Being on the security detail not only allowed Tende to meet people in other countries to do business with, it also got him all the special perks of the ruling party. So, in addition to fighting about impromptu trips, I was passive aggressive about his service to the party that had run the country into the ground.

The uncomfortable conversation of the relationship.

I did not mind the travelling. It was the trips that snuck up on me that I did not like. Tende had missed our anniversary weekend, my work Christmas party and our first house viewing, all because a minister called and he dropped everything. Outside of that, I liked the space and how it allowed me to see my friends and work just enough.

Takunda had similar convictions about Tende as those of my mother, and she had never met him. It was strange to me that she wanted to talk about my love life at all because that was just not the relationship we had. It was uncharted territory but in my good spirits, I decided I would humour her.

"So does he want kids?"

"You and your mother are obsessed with children."

Why did everyone want more children? She had four running around. Was that not enough for the whole family?

"Tell me this, what did you say you're using for your face?"

"What?"

"Well?"

"Nothing. Soap."

"Thought so."

"What?"

"I asked if Tendekai wants children because you are glowing like you're pregnant."

Once bitten twice shy also applies to raw sex apparently.

"I am not a doctor, I just have eyes. But maybe consider seeing one."

The thought of being pregnant had given me anxiety since I found out what it took to no longer be pregnant. I wanted so little do with it, the idea was far-fetched. I was not alarmed by my sister's observation, because even I saw improvements in my skin over the last year and it had nothing to do with a baby. Glowing skin was indicative of happiness and a healthy skin routine. Tende and I were not exactly being careful. I did not want to take any more contraceptives and we never wore condoms. We always said we would sit down and agree on the method we would use forever, but when it was time to fuck logic flew out the window and our interim method was yet to let us down. If there was the slightest chance that I was pregnant, I knew the distance had a part to play, and I would have traced it back to the exact trip that caused it.

A few weeks prior to Tende taking a trip to Johannesburg that went on for three weeks, and the night he arrived back, I made sure we made up for it. It was the first time in one year and five months in our time together that he had come inside me. We had spoken about moving in together and finding a house that night. We looked at the bathrooms we hated and the kind of master bedroom we needed to fit our clothes. We talked about getting an apartment with two bedrooms so he could have a home office once the travelling stopped. We had a vision. Our emotions got the best of us that night. The conversation we had thereafter was short. I had been quick to remember the first argument we ever had. And so had he, because all he asked as he stared at the ceiling was

"Do you wanna take it?"

I did not need to ask what, because I knew he meant the pill.

"I will."

"Okay. I will never make you do anything you don't wanna do."

27

"TJ if you do not stop that right now... *Wakufarisa! You're getting too excited!* I am so sorry girl."

She apologised for the third time, taking me out of the trance I found myself in. Her toddler had taken interest in my handbag and played with the straps on the chair next to mine where it sat free, because there were plenty of chairs to go around. I welcomed the distraction, not that I really needed it. I sat in the reception of Dananai's Women's Clinic a few days after Takunda left Harare, and waited through lunch hour for the gynaecologist to tell me I was not pregnant. I had been sure it would have been the worst deja vu yet. But it was nothing like going to the healthcare centre at my university. Things were different.

I was different.

I did not have the anxiety that sat on my chest or the ball of grief that usually moved up and down my throat when I was in pain. My period was only two days late, which was not strange. That biological norm put my mind at ease. Since making the appointment, my mind had taken me back to the waiting area of the Johannesburg General Hospital. It was two years later and I was sure I could not go through that kind of physical pain again. I wondered if I hated the pain enough to have a child if I was pregnant. It scared me that I did not have the answer. My strong convictions about marriage and children were beginning to be challenged. I did not think I was ready, but the closer I got to the future, the more I told myself it might not be so bad if the person I did it with was Tende. He was so good to me. So sure. Tende had surprised me while Takunda was still in Harare. He showed up at my door with a diamond necklace for me and flowers for my sister. The three of us went on a lunch date before he took us on a drive along Harare's longest road and headed into a complex of luxury garden flats.

"You are basically the king of surprise viewings."

I laughed immediately. I was nervous because I had not told Takunda, who sat in the backseat of Tende's Mercedes with her head titling and eyes bulging out of her skull, that Tende and I were looking for places to live. There was no way to say those words without talking about marriage. I was also nervous because this was by far the nicest looking complex we had visited. My fully furnished apartment was comfortable, but it was in the city center and had no garden. It was nothing in comparison to what I was looking at. The gate was tall and each flat was a double story with perfectly cut grass and an assortment of flowers where a stoned path led to the main doors. I already knew the only thing I could afford if we ever lived there would be groceries and even that would be pointless because Tende bought those too.

"No, my love. I am the king of surprises. Surprise!" He handed me an envelope and a key.

"Ours for the year. You do not even have to breathe in the same room as the agent." It was a recurring joke we made that there was no group of people I hated more than estate agents. And now I could live in this expensive apartment and move in without paying a cent or worrying about a single thing.

A whole fucking apartment?

"Sorry, what?" I was already crying and I did not know why. My sister was screeching and getting out of the car encouraging Tende to do the same.

"*Pazoita Mukwasha manje*! You have found another son for our mother!" Her voice high pitched with excitement.

"T." He called and my stare switched between the envelope that now sat in my hand and Tende who now stood at the driver's door with my sister wondering why I had not said a word.

A whole fucking apartment.

***

Tende set alight something in me. I experienced what love through money looked like and it made everything easy. I found myself imagining what it might be like to sit in that apartment with Tende. My resolve dwindled slowly in the days that led to the gynaecologist appointment. My mind was consumed with all the ways my life could end up that might make me happy, even though I did not plan for it. I set the appointment half-heartedly knowing my period was irregular when big changes happened in my life. I arrived at the clinic at the beginning of lunch hour and had to wait longer than usual because my appointment was only for 2.30pm. The reception was spacious with a large television on the wall, and chairs that surrounded the room's four walls. There was a large wooden table that sat in the middle of the room and carried a large vase of white flowers and magazines. I sat a few chairs away from the woman who fetched me from my train of thought and the child she referred to as TJ.

"That's okay no need to apologise." I responded

She had been the first face I noticed walking in because she was astoundingly beautiful. Her pregnancy looked good on her. She could have pulled off anything though, because she was perfect. Her skin was dark and her eyebrows sat perfectly arched without a sign of a brow pencil. Her hair was blonde and cut close to her scalp. She had a nose ring and wore a matte nude lipstick. The two of us had been sitting in the reception of Dananai Women's Clinic for about 45 minutes when the nurse told us the genealogist would only be back in another hour.

"They are a handful! Girl, after this one I am done!" She cradled her stomach. She did not look like she had a child before the one that sat in her stomach. I was sure after she gave birth she would not look like she had two.

"Are you here for Dr Mugarire as well?" she asked me.

"Yea. First time, I hope he is good." I replied.

"The best. You should definitely use him for all your pregnancies; he is hands on. Assuming you are pregnant, you could be here for a pap smear. Girl. Sorry." She looked embarrassed and started to laugh.

"I talk too much. It's what happens when you are always alone with a toddler."

"That's okay. Do you have a helper?" I liked her. She was friendly. She reminded me of my friends.

She reminded me of me.

"Have to. I work full time and my husband puts in hours like a dog. Not that I am complaining." She waved her left hand to show the massive diamond that sat on her wedding finger. In those five minutes I had decided I more than liked her. I wished she was my friend. If I had a ring like that, I would have shown it to the woman next to me too.

"Damn, sis. What's the secret?" I laughed.

I love black women.

"A big heart and a fat pocket."

I love bad bitches.

The half hour that followed was filled with the banter and chat about children, marriage and good neighbourhoods. She told me about never having wanted marriage or children until her husband came along. That their relationship was different to her somehow and it made it all worth it. I was reluctant to share with her, but I told her I was unsure if I was pregnant.

"Well does he know you are here?" She asked after I told her my suspicion.

"Not yet." I had not told Tende where I was. I needed to process my own feelings, even if I was pregnant, he was going to know when I knew what I wanted.

"Well you seem happy to talk about him so maybe this whole situation will surprise you. My man is squeamish and cannot stand the sight of blood, but he did not leave my side in labour and he does not leave my side about the baby. Though he is late today."

I wondered if she was right. She got into my head. Her cute baby, the big rock and her love story played in my head like a supercut. In those few minutes I started to envision those things for myself. It was different when there was an example right in front of you. I knew there was no way her and I were similar to the T, but it was close enough. She was opinionated, educated and attractive. She looked happy perched up on the chair, in embrace of her marital and maternal life. My eyes found themselves on her rock and then back on my own hands. Tende would buy a rock like that. Something worth a fortune and hard to miss.

Big heart and a fat pocket right?

"Got you thinking?" she interrupted my train of thought. My face gave away that things were happening in my head at lightning speed.

"A little bit." I nodded slowly as I shared a look with her.

God she was beautiful.

"Come TJ daddy's here!" she exclaimed as she placed her phone down and reached her arms out for the toddler to leave my handbag alone. I stared at his little hands fiddle with the straps and envisioned one his size crawling around at our new apartment. Something about Tende made me sure he would be a good father someday.

"Sorry I am late babe you know these Ministers."

"It's okay daddy hiiiii."

"Tende?"

***

The Enlightenment

In 2014 I sat in Barret 1 at Rhodes University, in a Politics 201 lecture with my best friend Kim and we talked about which term essays we would be doing. When it was my turn to tell I said:

"Not feminism. How boring."

Kim responded "Oh, definitely not!" And we continued with our lives. I do not know why I said that, because I never attended my Politics lectures so how could I have possibly known what feminism was or was not, enough to make an academic decision on it? The power of misinformation. It was not the equality I hated, it was the label because I was misinformed and misinformed about being misinformed. I had started to actively question society by the time I had this exchange with Kim. It was an early stage of my learning when I had only one toe in the water to test the temperature.

Occasionally, I wish that had happened sooner so I could take advantage of great experiences like writing theoretical essays on feminism. But other times I am at peace because my consciousness is a result of collective experiences and teachings of other black women I encounter. And while academia and all its whiteness gave me context through reading and contributing, it did not awaken the voice within me that is in perpetual protest of inequality. I cannot explain it because my memory fails me, but when I think of growing up I think of myself watching things happening around me. I think of all the little things I hated then and I hate them now except now I know why. When I was a child, we visited the rural area every other weekend. It was close by and people enjoyed unity. I never understood why only men could have the thigh or the drumstick of a chicken. Or why the men could not wash their own hands outside. The time it took one woman to kneel before every man, washing and drying his hands, could have been used to get the food out faster.

The older I grew the more I observed, the more I feared and the closer I came to this state of mind. In my teenage years I wondered why the boys hugged each other after one of them kissed a girl, but their girlfriends who came back to the hostel were told they had been used. I attended a high school where the teachers were mean, hateful and judgemental I can confidently say. Maybe they had their reasons. But I never understood why hugging a boy meant I would fall pregnant, ruin my life and die. Why did I always have to be ashamed? I had only been in university a few months before I started to resent that every man I experienced wanted me to prove how deserving I was. If I could cook? If I was old fashioned? The way I had 'given' something after sex instead of shared it, the way I was ashamed to say I had not felt pleasure.

The suffocation of it all. It radicalised me. I had to be exceptional and men could just be. I saw it in lectures, when I went out with my friends, at sports events, it was inescapable and the more I experienced it, the more I wondered how this had taken so long. This enlightenment of my place in the world and how it informed everything else. The enlightenment that then forged my path, professionally, intellectually, mentally and emotionally. What this looked like around 2014 in my second year of university is that I slowly followed my instincts. Slower than I am happy with now, but bit by bit I said what I thought about things even when I was afraid it might make people uncomfortable. I started realising they were denying me that same courtesy when they made it necessary for me to speak up about the rape joke, the sexual harassment or the slut shaming. I started to separate myself from those people and those places completely, but patriarchy is everywhere, even in death you can't escape it.

I tried to surround myself with people I could learn from. I would look at my social media and wonder how other women were so articulate, intelligent and passionate about feminism. Something evolved in me. Pictures of what I did not want became clearer. I had a fight in me. I still have it. It can never run out because it is fuelled by my experiences that remind me every day that I am a woman. My rebellion seeped into every part of my life and changed the way I saw love too. Finding myself did not protect me from heartbreak or any other emotional discomfort that came with the complexity of human interaction. It did not stop me from falling short and even now raging in my feminism, I continue to stumble because I am human.

There are decisions I made long after questioning the order of things and my actions did not reflect that. I could confidently criticise those actions today knowing I will never make them again, but I see why another woman might. I wish that every feminist experiences people with the ability to see beyond their own experiences because that is empathy, and there is no love or this movement without it. I now see myself in every woman and I want it all for us, across class and identity. To write these words alone is a dream. Something that T who sat in the healthcare centre of University of Witwatersrand would have never thought. One that T who sat in the car with Neill after he took money from her wallet could even think to wish for. Especially not one T who sang for choir in the library with radicalism brewing in her. She would never have imagined the accolades would read Tinatswe Mhaka: Storyteller.